Cheers for Screwball

In her debut novel, SCREWBALL, Keri Mikulski has covered all the bases. This is an exciting story. Spunky Ashley finds herself out of her league, facing tough competition on both the sports and romance fronts. Does first love win out, or does Ashley sacrifice it all to pursue her softball dreams? I laughed, I cried, and I cheered for Ashley. So will you.

Angela De Groot

Children's Author

Screwball is a high school romance that won't leave you hanging in left field. From softballs to slime balls---follow Ashley as she copes with being an athlete, handling mean girls, and having a boyfriend.

Colleen Rowan Kosinski

YA Author

I loved this book and I don't even play softball!

Taylor Gray

Eighth Grader

ISBN 978-0-9796908-0-8

Screwball

AN ASHLEY CLARKE NOVEL

BY: KERI MIKULSKI

To: Kaci Olivia

Top of the First
September, Freshman Year

I've never been so nervous in my life. Not horrible, like a shot at the doctor's office nervous, but more of a jumping into the deep end of a pool kind of nervous.

Coach D turns around and looks at me. This is it. I know it. She says, "Ashley, warm up."

A tingle runs down my spine at the same time my stomach drops with the words I dread, but I'm also dying to hear.

Strangers on the bench lean forward to get a good look at me, the newbie. A trio of teammates whisper to each other.

I reach for my glove and meander over to the ball bucket.

"Christy, grab a mask and warm her up," Coach D orders.

Turning around, I see Christy's shoulders droop as she shuffles over to her glove and slowly eases off her jacket. Her dark auburn ringlets spill out of a high ponytail while she maneuvers an orange Crush visor above her ears.

"Hi, Chrissy, I'm Ashley." I speak without making eye contact with my new teammate.

"My name is Christy," she responds. Her icy crystal-blue eyes pierce mine.

I follow her out of the dugout to the other side of the outfield fence.

"Hey, how long have you been playing for the Crush?" I ask, attempting to both break the ice and make up for the name screwup. It fails worse than the math test I took on Friday.

Christy barrels ahead of me. No answer.

As I begin my typical warm up, I think about how I got myself into this mess.

About a week ago, Kate, my jock BFF since micro mini soccer, approached me during fifth period. "Hey, my ASA team needs a pitcher. Our back-up just moved," she said.

"I have a team," I said without hesitation.

"You know we're a better team. Anyway, Ashley, you're a freshman now, you should be playing on a sixteen and under team."

One call from Kate's dad to mine and whoolah, I'm here on a new team with new girls. Dad thinks this is a great opportunity for me. I think it sucks to be new.

"It's time for you to move on, Ashley. If you have a chance to play on a sixteen and under team at fourteen, it will only help you to improve your pitching. Better competition, better players behind you, blah, blah, blah," he went on and on for at least an hour.

Even though I know it's better for my future to play with sophomores and juniors, right now I miss my friends on my old team. I liked that feeling of knowing where I stood on the team.

Pop.

I rotate my arm and complete my warm-up with my arsenal of pitches – drop, screw, curve, change-up, and my newest, the rise. My screwball is my go-to pitch. I love the way it jolts. But, my change-up is a close second. With an almost sixty mile-per-hour fastball, my change-up is knee-buckling.

"I'm done," I announce. Christy hasn't said a word to me throughout the entire warm-up. I ponder what her problem is as I jog back to the bench.

Glancing over her shoulder, Coach D asks me if I'm ready to go.

"Yup." I can feel my hands begin to tremble.

"Time-out." Coach D calls.

Adrenaline pumps through my body.

Jogging to the pitcher's mound, I try to settle the butterflies fluttering around in my stomach by reminding myself that I have pitched a bazillion times before this. What's one more inning? So what if it's a really good team and I'm brand new - I belong here.

Kate, Emily (the catcher), and the other infielders, meet me on the mound with Coach D. Coach D grabs the ball from Missy, the starter, and hands it to me.

"Okay, Ashley. The score is 3-2, us. Runners are on second and third. Keep the ball low and let's win this game. Remember, we picked you to do this. We chose you because you are an awesome pitcher." Coach D attempts to build my confidence.

"Are your signs the same?" Emily anxiously asks me.

We run through the signs quicker than I can text message. "Cool." Relief sweeps over Emily's face.

I dig my foot into the mound making it more familiar. I try to block thoughts out of my head, such as Andrew, my brand new boyfriend, sitting in the bleachers.

Poor Andrew. I hope my parents haven't scared him off by now. I so want him to see me save this game. I'll show him he's not the only athlete at Sunray High School.

I take in a deep cleansing breath, relax my shoulders, receive the sign from Emily, begin my windup, wrist snap, and release.

Pop!

I'm in the zone.

"Strike."

I take another sign from Emily. We are practically reading each other's minds. I nod, find the seams, and wind up.

Pop!

"Strike."

Great 0-2. Just the way I like it. With my confidence building with every pitch, I check the runner on third.

This is it. If I get this batter out, we win the game.

Another sign. I wind up again and release a change-up.

Dong.

The batter stops her swing midway through to handle the pitch. A dribbler barely reaches the mound. Quickly, I grab it with my bare hand and whip it to Maggie at first.

"Out!"

Cheers erupt from the stands. We win 3-2, leaving runners at second and third.

"Nice save." Emily says to me on our way to the dugout.

Jogging by, Kate smiles, "I told you, you would love the team."

Love the team? Sure, I feel amazing after saving the game. But, love the team? I wouldn't go that far. I love my old team, my old friends, and teammates that talked to me when we warmed up.

After slapping hands with the other team and receiving some more praise from my new teammates, we gather in left field.

"Nice job today," Coach D congratulates us. "Ashley, fantastic save. We'd like to officially welcome you to the team."

The girls clap. I smile and look down at the grass. My cheeks are hot because I totally hate that feeling when all eyes are on me. It's weird it doesn't bother me when I'm pitching. I guess because I'm concentrating and in my zone and don't even notice. But in front of everyone, and in the spotlight, I despise it.

"We still have a couple of things to work out. I'll see everyone at practice on Monday. Enjoy the rest of your weekend."

In unison, we stroll over to the dugout to gather our things. I feel good. As I look up, I notice Christy glaring at me. She's huddling with two other girls in the corner of the dugout. I swear I hear my name. What could they be talking about? Christy and her cronies turn around at the same time and stare at me.

My jaw tenses as I mentally run down the day. I don't think I said anything to piss them off. Should I say something now?

I peer out of the dugout and catch a glimpse of Andrew's dimples as he waits for me at the fence. Christy flies out of my head, instantly replaced by his gorgeous smile.

Bottom of the First
September, Freshman Year

I reach my destination, Andrew. My parents and little bro, Max, swarm me like paparazzi stalking a celebrity.

"Nice finish, Ash." Andrew reaches out to carry my bag. What a gentleman.

Not only was I nervous about today's game, but to top it off, Andrew spent the day with my nerdy parents. I pull my fingernails with my teeth.

"Nice work," my dad adds as he adjusts his USA Softball Cap. "I knew you'd like the team."

Why does everyone think I like this team?

"Let's celebrate. Who wants ice cream?" shouts my mom while clapping her hands together to generate enthusiasm. I scan her choice of outfits today. A black Old Navy Halloween t-shirt and hip-hugging jeans. Not too bad. At least her hair is back to normal since the summer's Victoria Beckham hairstyle disaster. Actually, my mom's not too bad looking, I mean for a forty-something year old. At least she means well and probably didn't say much around Andrew. My Dad on the other hand, I'm sure totally bored Andrew with his softball babble.

"Ice cream, ice cream," Max chants, jumping up and down like he's on a trampoline.

I look at Andrew first. He's all smiles. "Okay. How about Danny's?" I ask.

"Great idea, Boo," my mom answers.

My face grows hot for the second time today. I glance up at Andrew, who smiles like the Joker. "My name is Ashley, mom. I'm not two. Please, stop calling me Boo."

Nail pulling instantly turns into nail chomping.

"LA Woman" by the Doors blares from my dad's mid-life crisis convertible as we spin out of the parking lot. Max squishes himself between Andrew and me in the back seat. My mom sings along with the radio as my dad attempts guy talk with Andrew.

"So Andrew, what will you be driving when you get your license?" my dad asks.

"I don't know, Officer Clarke. What was your first car?" he innocently asks over the blaring music and intermittent scanner sounds. He has no idea how totally long-winded my dad can get.

Sighing, I sink into the backseat that my dad probably cleaned with a toothbrush this morning. The leather seats are whiter than most people's teeth. I stare at Andrew. How the heck did I land such a hottie?

This past summer when I was traveling up and down the East Coast with my fun and stress-free fourteen and under team, my best friend Lizzy met this guy Mark at Cape Town Coffee House where she was working.

Lizzy's been my best friend since preschool. A total beauty queen, awesome athlete combo. But, unlike me, she doesn't really give a crap about sports. I swear Lizzy just plays sports to get a tan, have a great toned body, and throw down whatever food she wants.

My summer did not consist of blueberry bagels and balmy nights, but of softball and sliders. I think I threw about five thousand pitches total that summer.

When I returned from softball, Lizzy asked me to meet up with her and Mark. I was hesitant at first, since Lizzy has a history of using me as an excuse so she doesn't get down and dirty too soon. But, Lizzy begged me, and I didn't have anything to do, so I went.

We met Mark at Mario's Pizza. To my happy surprise, Mark brought smoking hot, junior sports legend at Sunray Beach High School, Andrew Sinclair.

Lizzy, Mark, Andrew, and I found a table and ordered a pie. With sauce dripping from my face, I tried to stay calm and tried even harder not to drool while I snuck peeks at Andrew.

"Crap," I grabbed a napkin.

"What's wrong with you?" Lizzy asked as Mark and Andrew looked at us.

"Nothing, it's nothing, Lizzy. I have to go to the bathroom," I gave Lizzy 'the look' and she followed me.

When we were safe from the guys' view, Lizzy asked, "What, do you have your period or something?"

I show Lizzy the giant red pizza stain on my crotch.

She cracked up. "You look like you do."

"Shut up and help me with this," I said as I continued to scrub the stain with a rough paper towel. Instead of a red stain, I had a giant wet stain on my pants. But, I couldn't stay in the bathroom all night, so we nonchalantly left the bathroom to join the group.

During my stroll to the table, I spied Mark's eyes survey to the trouble spot and widen. Great. So much for making a hot impression on Andrew.

We finished our pizza with no more interruptions. "Let's go to the beach," Mark suggested.

We all live on an island off the Southern Tip of New Jersey. The beach side is Sunray Beach. The bay side is Cape Town. Everyone on the island either attends Sunray Beach High School or Cape Catholic. Lizzy, Mark, Andrew, and I all attend Sunray Beach, even though Mark lives in Cape Town. When you live in a touristy area, it's crazy small in the winter and jammed packed with shoobies causing chaos in the summer.

Mark and Andrew took off ahead of Lizzy and me, shed their t-shirts, and dove into the ocean.

"Come on, it's warm," Mark shouted.

"No way," Lizzy yelled. I thought about jumping in considering my pants were already wet. But, I really liked the view of Andrew from the sand, so I stayed put.

The late sun shone off Andrew's glistening chiseled body. His tan six-pack abs looked hot.

"Stop drooling," Lizzy snapped her fingers. "Are you going to kiss him? I know he wants to kiss you."

"Slow down, Lizzy. I just met him!"

My cheeks were hotter than a mid-summer's day.

Swoosh. Andrew came up for air after he dove through a wave. He shook his head and ran his fingers through his sun-streaked dark hair. As he walked out of the surf he looked like he was walking right out of an Abercrombie and Fitch ad.

"You wanna walk?" Andrew asked me.

"Sure," I answered, secretly hoping my cheek color was back to normal.

He pulled a white tee over his head and it stuck to his chest.

"I heard you play softball," he said.

"Yeah, I heard you play football," I said. I scanned my brain for something else to say, but I was speechless.

"Yup. I can't believe we scrimmage already this weekend."

"What position do you play?" I asked.

"Quarterback."

A tingle ran through my body. This super hottie plays Brady Quinn's position. Brady Quinn was the quarterback for my all-time favorite college football team, Notre Dame, a couple of years ago. Now he's in the NFL playing for the Browns.

"Do you like playing quarterback?" I asked.

"Love it. I heard you pitch. How do you throw the ball like that?" Andrew stopped. With a horrible goofy motion, he attempted to pitch an invisible softball.

I began to explain how I throw a pitch. Andrew listened and even gave the motion another try.

When we were done with the mini lesson, he darted right and climbed the wooden lifeguard stand. Hoisting myself up the stand, I sat next to him. The scent of salt water and a faint smell of cologne filled the air. He leaned forward, placed his elbows on his knees, and ran his fingers through his damp hair.

He turned around and smiled. His teeth are perfect, gleaming white and straight. I pulled my legs to my chest. Andrew's so beautiful. This is nuts. I'm just a freshman.

The wind picked up. He looked into my eyes, lifted his hand, and moved a flyaway hair that was tickling my nose behind my ear. He cupped his smooth hands on my face, moving closer to me. Andrew's so confident. I'm so not.

His soft full lips hit mine. He kissed me gently. As I kissed him back, I tasted a combination of salt water and peppermint.

Gently, he pulled away, smiled, and hugged me. Releasing my legs from my grip, I hugged him back as I steadied myself on the bench.

I cherish that day like my mom relishes the days Max and I were born. I can recite each and every detail, from Andrew's smell to what I felt like when he kissed me. That day changed my life. I was no longer Ashley Clarke, the jock; I was Ashley Clarke, Andrew Sinclair's girlfriend.

Just thinking about that night makes me smile as Andrew and my dad carry on their car conversation. I mean, how is it possible that Andrew Sinclair wants to hang out with me? Ashley Jean Clarke. The girl who spends every second slinging a softball. The girl who only kissed one other boy in seventh grade after a pick up basketball game, which doesn't really count because we only did it because we both wanted to get the first kiss thing over with. I reach out and touch Andrew's hand. He looks at me and grins.

Our tires kick up stones as we pull into Danny's Double Dip Ice Cream.

"Boo, are you having your usual?" my mom asks.

Andrew chuckles.

I throw my hands in the air and roll my eyes.

My parents stroll, hand in hand, over to the ice cream stand as Max weaves in and out of the line of customers. Andrew and I stand back to catch a couple of seconds alone.

"Awesome job today," Andrew says as I slide my hand in his.

"Thanks." A shiver runs up my spine.

"Mom, look, Andrew is holding Ashley's hand. Eeeeww-ww," shouts Max.

My family is seriously annoying me as they make their way to the front of the line and lick their cones before Andrew and I decide what we want.

"Ice cream's on us, for the superstar of the game." My dad says in between licks of chocolate. He hands Andrew a ten.

With my freaky family busy licking away by the car, Andrew and I are in the clear; we step up to the window to order.

"A chipwich." I tell the petite blond in itty-bitty shorts and an even tinier top that tries to contain the two mountains popping out. I glance at Andrew and notice his eyes are taking in the mountain view. I look down at my orange slider, matching scrunched up socks, and shiny shorts. I am a giant pumpkin. You know, I never noticed the competition until I landed one of the hottest guys at Sunray Beach High.

"I'll have... let's see." Andrew says.

Is it me or is he stalling to hang out longer with the Pam Anderson body double?

"What do you suggest?" Andrew says finally bringing his eyes up to the girl's face.

The tiny blond smiles showing teeth whiter than my dad's

upholstery and giggles. "You can have whatever you want," she answers coyly.

My parents, thank God, are oblivious to this flirtation. They are too busy enjoying Danny Dip's Famous Ice Cream and can't hear over the oldies blaring from the convertible.

I bite my lip and clench my fists, ready to shove my ice cream up blondie's butt.

After what seems like an eternity, Andrew finally makes a decision. She whips up our orders. "Bye," she chirps as she waves like Miss America to Andrew, totally ignoring me.

I gnaw on the edges of my chipwich. Andrew licks his chocolate custard sugar cone like nothing happened as we find a bench as far away from my parents as possible. I'm so new to this relationship thing. Should I say something or let it go? Am I being insecure?

I try to be cool, but I can't stand it anymore. "Was that really necessary?"

"What are you talking about?"

"That girl. You were flirting with her."

"I was not. Relax, you spaz."

Was I imagining things? Am I just insecure because Pam over there looks great and I'm covered with grass stains and orange dirt? I dust some dirt off my arm and look over at Andrew. Maybe I do need to relax. I mean, so what if some chick thinks he's hot. Girls are going to think he's gorgeous because he totally is and

I really need to learn to deal.

Andrew gently smiles at me as he tosses the last piece of cone into his mouth.

Top of the Second
September, Freshman Year

When I get home, I instantly log onto MySpace. Although, Andrew is always a nice diversion, Christy is still on my mind. Not on my mind, like I have a huge girl crush on her or anything, but in another way. Like I can't stop thinking about Christy's obvious weird hatred thing with me. I don't even know Christy; yet, I have to find out what this chick's problem is. That is if I decide to stay on the Crush.

First, I type in Christy Mayer. Nothing. Then, Christy, Cape Town Orange Crush, nothing. So, I try C Mayer. An explosion of orange, fastpitch videos, pictures, and friends fill Christina Mayer's screen. Softball is Christina's life. I watch the videos, scan the pictures, and scroll through her friends. Stephanie's and Amy's, the girls who were whispering with her at the field, faces splash all over her page. Best friends? I check out her blog. Nothing particular, mostly softball. Should I add a comment?

Hey, Christy. Lovin' the Crush so far. See you Monday. I delete it.

Never mind.

I do notice that a Mark from Sunray Beach High School is one of her friends. And there are a ton of comments about a Mark. Could this be Lizzy's Mark? Does Lizzy know?

I shut down the computer and text Andrew before I climb into bed, exhausted from a big day.

To: Andrew

Thanx 4 goin 2 my game.

9/07   10:13 p.m.

The next day, I catch a moment with Kate at her locker before homeroom. She practically whips me with her pale blond ponytail when I tap her on the shoulder.

"What's up, Ash?" she asks. "By the way, you pitched a great game yesterday."

"Thanks. I was wondering if you could fill me in on the team," I say trying to sound as nonchalant as possible.

Kate closes her locker to face me. "The team is great, loads of fun."

"What about the girls?" I ask hoping she'll offer up the info on Christy.

"Oh, they're great too," she smiles.

I give up. "What about Christy?" I ask.

I switch my tote to my other shoulder so I can bite my nail.

"What about her?"

"Uh, what's her deal?"

"Nothing. I know she worked all summer and juggled ASA. She's dedicated. Goes to Cape Catholic and hangs out with Stephanie and Amy all the time. Her grandmother comes to a lot of the games. That's all I know," she answers. "Is something the matter?"

A loud buzzing fills the hallway. Students scatter to their next class.

I stop mid nail chomping.

"No, nothing. I was just wondering," I say. "Have a good one." I start trekking to homeroom.

"Oh, duh, I almost forgot to mention," Kate says.

I swing around.

"She's the other pitcher, besides you. Her back's been bothering her. That's why she didn't pitch yesterday."

Figures. Why wouldn't Kate mention this before? Did she know I'd have a problem with Christy?

I let out a sigh and walk toward my homeroom. So, Christy not only has some weird ties to Mark and Andrew, but she pitches too. I'm screwed.

"Hey, Ashley." Andrew pecks me on the cheek.

Ever since the summer, we're inseparable, and I love every minute of it.

"I got your text this morning." Andrew looks at me with his big brown eyes. "I love going to your games."

I smile. What more could a girl want?

"Andrew, do you know Christy Mayer," I ask. It's worth an attempt.

His face turns from sweet to surprised. "Why?"

"Uh, she's on my new team."

What does he mean, "Why?"

"Mark lives near her in Cape Town. Grew up with her or something," he says. "See you later, gotta go."

Andrew walks down the hallway. I turn into homeroom.

That was cryptic.

I fall into my hard, cold chair. Jake Cole is chatting up two Goth chicks in all black in front of me. Jake is the polar opposite of Andrew. Bad boy, dark, wiry, crazy, but totally one of my best guy friends. He's got this positive happy vibe going for him. Everyone, especially the girls, love hanging out with him.

"Hey, beautiful," he turns around. "When are you going to dump that pretty boy and date a real man like me?"

"Whatever, Jake. When are you going to stop messing around with every girl on this island?" The Goth girls give me a strange look as they slink out the door. I hope they don't cast a spell on me later with a voodoo doll or something.

"I don't discriminate. I mess around with Mainland girls too. And anyway, what are you? Jealous?"

I burst into giggles.

He's been teasing me forever. What a screwball.

"Did you do your English homework?" he asks after we stop laughing. Jake opens up his notebook and grabs a pencil off the floor.

"Maybe," I tease.

The bell rings and the Pledge of Allegiance screams through the loudspeaker.

"Don't forget the Homecoming Dance is drawing near. If you want to help out with the dance committee, stop by Mrs. Miller's room, E15." The speaker drones on and on.

Bottom of the Second
October, Freshman Year

"Did Andrew ask you yet?" Lizzy quizzes me as we change into our mismatched gym clothes.

"Nope."

"What? The dance is only two weeks away." Lizzy smoothes down her brand new honey-blonde highlights and maneuvers herself in front of the mirror to apply lip gloss.

"I guess he's just waiting for the right time." I answer. But, deep inside I've been sweating this for a while. Why hasn't he asked me? I mean, we have been together for two whole months. We spend every free minute with each other.

The whole decision has me stressed out to the max. I have a fall ball tournament three hours away, the last one this season, the same weekend as the homecoming game and dance.

"Are you scaring him off with your jockstrap?" Lizzy laughs.

"Here, Ash, put some lip gloss on." She comes at me with her weapon of girliness.

I playfully push her away. "Shut up, Liz."

She hip-checks me as we hustle through the swinging door to gym class. We find our spots on the basketball court to do our usual half-ass stretch routine with Mr. Butcrick. Some names are just so wrong.

I'm feeling a little irritated that I didn't catch a glimpse of Andrew during gym class. We share the same period. On a good day, our classes are both playing football at the same time on adjacent fields. Oh well, we're still playing soccer and his class must be running the track finishing those corny Presidential fitness tests. What a joke.

Every year, I ace every category besides flexibility. I'm a three-sport athlete, but dancer and cheerleader chicks always end up winning that stupid fitness medal while I'm stuck trying to touch my toes.

After gym class, Lizzy and I stroll down the hallway toward our lockers. Andrew catches up with me and grabs my arm.

"Hey," he says as he gently pulls me over to the side of the hallway. "Do you want to come over tonight after your game? I have something to ask you," he says.

Butterflies flutter.

I know this is it. He's going to ask me to the dance. Finally!

Before I have a chance to answer him, three senior blondes approach us.

"Hey, Andrew. Are you ready?" The one that looks like that Playboy chick, Kendra, from "The Girls Next Door" purrs as she smoothes her poker straight locks.

"Just a second," he answers.

Ready for what?

The girls stroll off and wait by the Science lab door.

"So, I'll see you tonight, right?" He pecks me on the lips. The girls stare at us.

"Yeah, I can't wait." I try hard not to sound as insecure as I feel. This is my first boyfriend. Should I be pissed he's hanging out with Kendra, Holly, and Bridget wannabes? Or am I being a big dork because all he's really doing is going to class?

I watch the girls surround Andrew like Hugh Hefner. Why do I feel so out of emotional control around him? Urgh.

I pull on my yellow Sunray Beach soccer jersey as I run the play by play of the Playboy bunny episode by Lizzy.

"Why do you think he would want to be with those girls?" Lizzy asks.

"I don't know. Maybe, because they're hot, more girlier than me, have boobs. Do I have to continue?"

"Did he ever give you a reason not to trust him?"

"No, not yet." I answer.

"Right, so until he does, you really have no choice but to trust him. Unless, you want to break up with him."

"No way," I say.

I know Lizzy is right, but I still wonder.

"And anyway, Ash, you have a big tournament that same weekend, remember? Maybe you shouldn't go over to his house. You know he's going to ask you to the dance. Then what are you going to do?" Lizzy brushes her hair and applies more globs of mascara.

But, I want him to ask me. I want to know he cares and likes me.

After the soccer game and another easy win, we load onto our yellow bus. Too much yellow. Sunray Beach High, sunshine pride. Who ever heard of a sun as the mascot? Watch out, we'll burn you with our heat.

The fall season is so busy. Between soccer and fall ball, I'm running constantly. It sucks. Plus, Sunray is a huge soccer school, so during the fall, the pressure is on.

I grab my phone from my drawstring bag and flip it open. One text from Andrew.

Fr: Andrew

C u 2 night

10/5/07   **5:15 p.m.**

"Thanks, mom." I lean over and peck my mom on the cheek as I practically bounce out of the car in front of Andrew's house.

"Bye, honey. Call me for a ride," my mom shouts.

Andrew's cell phone is glued to his ear. He's rocking on a wooden chair on his front porch. He pulls the phone from his ear when he sees me and flips it closed.

"Hey, Ash. How was your game?" he asks.

"Good. We won."

It's funny, when I ask Andrew about a football game, he runs the play-by-play by me, like an announcer. Whenever he asks me, I just tell him who won and what the score was. I have to speak enough play-by-play with my dad.

"What do you want to do?" he asks.

What do I want to do? I want you to ask me to the dance.

I smile my best mirror-practiced smirk and act coy. "Whatever."

"Come on in," he says.

I follow him into the house. We walk through the huge wooden door. Shiny hardwood floors spread out before me and a plush green carpeted spiral staircase is to the right off of a never sat in sitting room. Andrew's house is humongous.

"Want to hang out on the deck? It overlooks the bay."

I can't stop scanning the black and white portraits of Andrew, his sister, and parents on the beach, Andrew, as a baby, as a toddler, and now. My nosiness gets the better of me because I don't even hear Andrew. I'm too busy checking out the room like it's a museum and I'm on a field trip.

"Ashley, what are you doing?" Andrew asks after a couple of minutes of silence.

"Uhh. Just looking at pictures," I say as I pull myself to a standing position.

I look at Andrew. His hands are in the pockets of his jeans and his feet are fidgeting. Is he nervous? He's going to ask me tonight, I know it.

Andrew leads me through the kitchen, dining room, family room, through the sliding glass door.

I walk onto the deck and squint my eyes. The sun is setting and giving off this weird autumn glare.

During the bus ride to the game today, I pictured this moment. Just like MTV's "Laguna Beach", I'm sure Andrew slaved all week to make a perfect seashell letter phrase to spell out, "Will you go to the homecoming dance with me?" right there on the sand.

I would see it, read it, jump into his arms and say, "Yes." We would kiss as the water splashed onto our feet and over the perfectly laid out seashells. The sun would set as the camera faded.

I scan the beach. I don't see the seashells. In fact, all I see is a bunch of seaweed.

Andrew stretches out on a lounge chair.

"So, Ashley. How's softball? That was awesome how you

saved the game the other day."

"Thanks," I say. I slump down into a navy and white cushy chair.

"Isn't the bay calming? I kind of like the bay better than the ocean. It's so quiet. I can come out here to think, you know. Especially after a game."

"Yeah." I dig my palm into my cheek.

"Do you want to go to the dance with me?"

"What?" I say. Did he really just ask me this important question like he asked me if I wanted pizza or a hamburger the other day at lunch? I mean, even Mark asked Lizzy with a friggin' rose.

"Do you want to go to the homecoming dance with me?" he asks again.

"Sure," I say. I sit up straight hoping Andrew will walk over to me to give me a kiss or something a little romantic.

Instead, Andrew stares at the sea.

"I like hanging out with you, Ash. You make me feel so calm. Like, I can really be myself."

Yeah, your boring self, I think. But, then I look at Andrew. His golden skin, beautiful brown eyes, and full lips.

"Really? What do you mean?" I say.

"I mean, I could say something goofy and you wouldn't care. You're here to hang out with me, not use me like a trophy. Girls do that, you know. They think, "He's the quarterback, I want him." That's so stupid. I don't have to worry about that with you. You like me for me. Plus, you like to talk about sports. You're like a guy and a girl. A guy I can talk sports with and a girl that's hot and stuff."

Okay, it's not poetry, but he's beginning to win me over again after that lame proposal. But, I do feel a tad guilty. I mean, why do I like Andrew? Am I like the other girls? Do I only like him because he's hot? I run my fingers through my hair, looking for split ends. He thinks I'm hot. I can think about the trophy thing later.

"Why don't you come over here?" He moves over to make room for me next to him on the lounge chair.

I get up to snuggle next to him. Maybe he's not romantic, but he is gorgeous. Tons of girls at Sunray would trade places with me in a heartbeat if they could.

I think about telling Andrew about the tournament, but before I can say the words, Andrew cups my chin and kisses my lips. I forget all about softball and kiss him back.

After what feels like only seconds the front door slams shut. We both jump and pull apart. We hear his parents in the other room. I stand up to fix my hair. Andrew smiles and sits on the side of the lounge chair.

Andrew grabs a football. "Want to have a catch?"

"Sure," I smile.

I take off across the sand. Andrew launches a perfect spiral to my outstretched hands. I grab it before it hits the bay.

He laughs as I stop myself from falling into the water.

I heave the ball back to him. He catches it and dives into the tiny wave. He's so goofy. Now, I'm laughing.

Maybe, he's right, we do make a good pair.

"Ash, are you okay?" Emily, the catcher, asks me as I begin my warm-up.

"Yeah, I'm fine." But I'm not fine really. I'm dragging from being up half the night hanging out at Andrew's and trying to decide what to do about the stupid dance.

I whip my arm, but my fastball isn't popping, and my pitches aren't moving. During the ride to the game this morning, oh man did I hear it.

"Was that you, Boo, up until three?" my mom asked me.

"Why do you care? I'm here, ready to play, aren't I?" I snapped back, irritated from my lack of sleep.

"Boo, boo, sissy, boo, boo," my little brother, Max, teased me.

"Shut up." I hissed.

My dad puts in his two cents. Obviously, this was a mom/dad tag team effort coordinated earlier. "Ashley, you're going to have to start making sacrifices if your goal is a softball scholarship."

Here we go, the ol' sacrifice speech. My dad droned on and on like the neighbor's non-stop barking dog.

"I know." I answered when he finally finished.

Smack.

Emily fires the ball back to me as I finish my warm-up.

Coach D makes her way over to us. "Ready to go, Ashley?"

"Yup. I'm ready." But, I'm not. I'm exhausted.

Captains and coaches are called, we go over our strategy, cheer, and I head to the mound. I love fall ball. The sun beats on your back, but its not summer sizzling. A cool breeze refreshes me as I grab the ball from the orange dirt.

I feel for the seams and locate my fastball and fire.

Smack.

Chalk puffs from Emily's glove.

Two pitches later, Emily fires a perfect strike to Kate, covering second. I receive the ball as the team meets me at the mound for our handshakes and cheer.

"Play ball," the umpire yells.

Emily gives the sign: curve ball, low outside.

I wind up and fire, but instead of the ball curving outside, it tails high. Emily dives to recover the wild pitch.

My body drags as I receive the ball from Emily. The batter takes signs from her coach, and digs in on the left side, this time for a drag. My infield moves in. Emily gives a screwball high sign. My best pitch.

I wind up and fire, miss my location, and the batter pops one right over the shortstop's head. She high-tails it to first before we even recover the ball.

One of Christy's crew, Stephanie, fires the ball back to me.

My teammates chant, "Get her at two."

The next batter receives her signs and digs in. Emily gives me the sign: low outside fastball. I wind up and fire. The ball hits the dirt; Emily explodes onto her knees and rips off her mask. Too late, speedy at first is already at second.

Emily launches the ball back to me. Another sign: inside fastball. I wind up and fire. The batter takes the perfect down the middle pitch and rips it to center. It flies over the center fielder's head, over the fence. Homerun.

I hang my head and mumble to myself. Down 2-0 with no outs.

Coach D calls time. "Are you okay, Ash?"

"Yeah, I'm fine." I lie. But, I'm not fine. I'm totally beat.

"Okay, girls, no big deal. Let's get three and get out of the inning. This girl hits up the middle. So, Kate and Brianna hug second," Coach D says.

We chant, "Team" together as Coach D jogs to the dugout.

Out of the corner of my eye, I see Christy get up, grab a ball, and walk out of the dugout to the bullpen.

Two more easy earned runs later, my infield miraculously gets me out of the nightmare inning.

As I jog into the dugout, I check the batting order. My name is crossed off replaced by Christy's.

"Take a rest, Ash, Coach D instructs me. "You look like you need it."

Finding the farthest spot from my teammates as possible on the bench, I slump and watch Christy dominate through six innings. We lose 4-0. Our name goes into the loser's bracket.

I stand up to find my bag.

Christy slaps her glove down on the bench next to me. Stephanie and Amy circle behind her like a pack of hungry wolves. Christy taunts, "Do you think you're really ready for sixteen and under? Aren't you like fourteen?"

I hear Christy's crew giggling.

"Maybe you're too young for this level, especially our team. You had one good game, Ash, but that was just luck. I heard Coach talking and you probably won't get another start for a long time." Christy says in between her croonies' muffled giggles. "Hello? Do you talk?" More giggles.

I don't know what to say. Maybe she's right. I shouldn't get another start after today. Eyes straight ahead, I continue to gather my things and pretend not to hear her. After what feels like an hour, Christy and her cronies finally finish with me and scatter to the snack stands.

When the coast is clear, I swing my bag over my shoulder feeling like a doormat.

I spot Kate a couple feet ahead of me. "Hey, Kate."

She turns around. "Hey, Ash. Tough one. You look a little beat. Long night last night?"

"Kind of."

"Don't let it get you down. No big deal. Anyway, the big tournament is Fall Brawl in two weeks," she says.

She joins her parents, and I find mine standing by a tree looking like they've been through their own brawl.

"You really sucked today," my brother says.

"Max," my dad says.

"So, did you learn a lesson, today, Boo?" is all my mom can muster at the moment.

"Don't start, mom." What I don't tell her is I did learn a lesson today. I learned softball is about sacrifices.

But, am I ready to sacrifice homecoming with hottie Andrew?

Top of the Third
October, Freshman Year

"What? Can't you go to the dance late?" Andrew looks up at me with his pups.

This sucks. Stressed to the max about this dance decision, I consider changing my mind about Fall Brawl. I've been playing like crap anyway, and I hate Christy. Digging my toes deeper in the sand, I let out a sigh.

"I tried, but my parents won't drive the extra six hours. Plus, we play early on Sunday. The hotels have been booked for months." Look at those yummy lips. Don't let the hotness sway you. Think softball.

"Homecoming is a big game, then the dance. It's a huge weekend. I wish you could be there." He wraps his thick arm around my shoulders.

"I know. Sorry." A cool autumn breeze cuts my skin.

"Cold?" Andrew takes off his hoody, my favorite gray sweat, with Sunray Beach Football written in raised letters. "You want to wear this?" he asks.

Yes, of course, I do.

I've been eyeing that sweatshirt for weeks. I love it.

"Okay." I answer. I pull the sweatshirt over my head and take in Andrew's slight cologne scent mixed with salt air. Yum. He will never see this sweatshirt again. Maybe I can't go to the dance, but at least I have his sweatshirt. A sweatshirt is so much better than some dumb dance corsage that dies like two days later.

He nuzzles my neck. Goose bumps cover my legs. He does it every time.

After some PG kanoodling on the beach, we stand by my front door. I decide to break the awkwardness of standing there with nothing to say after we totally made out for like hours with, "I had fun tonight."

"Me too," he says.

"I'll see you tomorrow," I say as I turn around.

He grabs my arm. "Wait."

I swing around to face him.

"It's okay if I ask one of my friends to the dance, right?" Andrew looks at his feet.

No, no, no. My stomach feels like I just took a fastball to the gut. I take a deep breath and manage to croak, "What?"

"Well, Ash, you don't expect me to be the third wheel with Mark and Lizzy, do you? Megan's been my friend since elementary school. She's like a sister. I told her about your game the other day when you were still deciding what to do and she mentioned us going as friends if you can't go." He meets my eyes.

Megan, the girl who, rumor has it, did some kind of different color lipstick thing with like five different guys from the football team? Sister, my ass. She's a slut.

"Do you mean Megan, the football team girl?" I ask hoping it's some other Megan.

"Ashley, that's not fair. The lipstick thing is a rumor. Megan's my friend. That's it." He takes a tiny step toward me.

Friend? Yeah, right. She's never been friends with a guy.

"This just feels weird, Andrew. I mean we're... Why can't you just go on your own?" I hug my arms around my chest and take a tiny step backwards.

"Everyone is going, Ash. Lots of people going as friends. Come here."

He takes me into his thick arms. My head sinks into his hard chest. I have to believe him. I don't want him to think of me as some crazy girlfriend. I can handle this. I mean, I'm strong. No biggie.

"I'm all yours, Ashley Clarke. You have nothing to worry about." He brushes the hair out of my eyes and gently kisses my cheeks, then my lips.

"Okay." I manage to croak.

After Andrew leaves, I race into my house and collapse on my bed. Looking up at the ceiling, all sorts of sordid dance scenarios flash through my head like television clips advertising the newest show. Andrew smiling holding Megan for pictures. Megan with her perfect body squeezed into a sexy dress. Andrew's hands on Megan's hips, gazing into her eyes, slow dancing to sappy love songs.

Tears trickle. I wipe them away leaving black splotches on Andrew's hoody. I hate softball right now. I hate that I have to go to a stupid tournament with a bunch of girls I don't even like while cheerleader Megan not only watches Andrew at the game, but also gets to go to the dance with him. I hate Megan for asking Andrew.

I stand up and march into the living room.

"I'm not going." I shout.

"What are you talking about?" my mom asks as she lays down the book she's reading.

"I'm not going to the Fall Brawl tournament." I place my hands on my hips.

"Where is this coming from? I thought you made a decision."

I did. But, things change. Like Megan and Andrew.

"I changed my mind." I answer.

"Does this have to do with Andrew? Did he break up with you because you can't go to the dance?"

She is so clueless. This isn't a hundred years ago.

"Did you hear me mom, I'm not going."

"The team is counting on you to win this tournament, Ash. You can't let everyone down. Besides, we already paid for the hotel room." Her voice grows louder with each word.

"What about me? Does anyone care that I can't go to a dance with my boyfriend?" I shout.

Mom rolls her eyes making me feel like a volcano ready to explode.

My dad strolls in to police our house like he does Cape Town. "Is everything alright?"

Here we go. He is not going to take this well. I clench, ready for my dad's outburst.

"Ashley doesn't want to go to the tournament." Mom blurts out.

"Ash, you have to go. This is ridiculous," my dad says waving his arms in the air.

"I'm sick and tired of softball. I've had enough. I need some time on my own. I'm sick and tired of missing stuff because I'm traveling with a bunch of girls, pitching day in and day out. I don't even like this team."

"Did Andrew break up with you?" my dad asks.

"Argh." I might as well talk to the wall. I stomp into my

room and slam the door. They just don't get it.

My blaring alarm clock wakes me. It's Friday, the day before the dance. Joy. I'm sure Andrew is pulling his football jersey over his head as Megan fluffs up her hair and wiggles into her cheerleading outfit.

The past ten days sucked. Like a tennis ball across a court I've flipped back and forth about the dance and tournament. But, I've made a promise to the team. Andrew's been overly nice, probably trying to erase any doubt in my mind about Megan and him. I roll out of bed and stumble to the bathroom to take a shower. I shut my eyes and try to think of sports instead of Megan's hands all over Andrew. Thank God, I have a soccer game after school today, so I don't have to think about this mess.

Dripping wet, I find my yellow jersey lying right where I left it last night. I grab it and change for this afternoon's pep rally, pairing it with jeans and slides. Paying particular attention to my hair and makeup, I think about the many ways I can torture Megan.

I flip my tote and duffle bag over my shoulder. "Bye." I say to my parents who are sitting at the table eating breakfast.

"No breakfast today?" my mom asks.

"Yeah, I'll grab something to eat on the way out." I say, secretly hoping they'll tell me it's okay if I miss the game.

"Remember what Aunty says, 'Boys are like buses. If you stand at the bus stop long enough, another bus just as good will come along','" my mom says.

What the hell is she talking about? Obviously, she thinks I'm about to give up softball for Andrew. Not softball, just one tournament. I grab a bagel off the counter.

School is cluttered with sunny decorations and uniforms. My stomach fights butterflies as I imagine what people are saying about Andrew taking Megan. "Is Ashley stupid? Why would she okay Andrew going to the dance with someone else?"

I spin my locker combination to the beat of Beyonce's "Irreplaceable" when Andrew grabs my waist.

He whispers in my ear. "Hey Ash."

I turn around to face him and take in the way his white football jersey hugs his broad shoulders. His sleeves are rolled up exposing his bulging biceps.

"Hey," I say.

"How's my number one girl?" He gently kisses my lips. For a moment, I forget all about the dance.

A couple of his teammates walk by us on their way to homeroom and smack him on his back. He turns around and grins for a split second, but keeps his attention on me the whole time.

"Ready for the big game?" I ask.

"Ready as I can be without my number one girl there."

"Andrew, we've been over this a hundred..."

"Hey Andy. What time do you want me to pick you up on

Saturday?" Bouncing over in her body hugging uniform is Megan.

My mouth drops. I turn my attention to my locker so I don't deck her. She's so close to Andrew's face, I couldn't even fit the novel I'm reading between them. Ugh, I hate her.

"How about seven?" Andrew asks.

"Can't wait. Oh hi, Ash. Don't worry I'll take care of Andrew for you." She purrs and turns to give Andrew a booty view as she bounces down the hallway to join the cheerleaders.

What does she mean she'll 'take care of Andrew for me?' Like she took care of the football team? I grab my Algebra book and stomp toward my homeroom.

"Ash, where are you going, homeroom doesn't start for another five minutes?"

I keep going, slump at my desk, and plunk my head down in between my crossed arms. This is going to be one long day.

"Hey, Ash. What's wrong, all this homecoming crap got you down?" Jake gently taps my shoulder.

I raise my head and adjust my ponytail.

"Let me ask you something, you're a guy."

I know Jake will be honest.

"If you had a girlfriend."

Jake giggles.

"No, really. If you had a girlfriend and your girlfriend couldn't go to the dance because she's playing sports, would you go with another girl, who happens to be a friend, to the dance?"

Jake's grin is a foot wide.

"What?" I ask. "Tell me. Would you?" I push his arm.

"You don't want to know what I think," he finally says.

"Yes, I do. Come on, Jake."

"All I'm saying is Andrew is quite a lucky guy. Dates a nice girl like you and gets to take a girl like Megan to a dance? How does he do it?"

Yuck. I totally don't like how I feel after hearing those words. I stare at Jake.

"Are you going to the dance?" I plaster a fake smile on my face, as I attempt to change the subject.

"Hell no. Dances are lame," Jake answers.

Saved by the bell. I swing around. As the announcements drone on, I think about what Jake said. Why don't I see it as clearly as Jake does? I mean, Andrew and Megan are just friends, right? So going to a dance together is no big deal. It's time for some major thinking about Andrew, and I've got plenty of time at the tournament this weekend.

"Will the freshman class please report to the gym for the pep rally?" the announcement echoes through the school.

I find Lizzy in the hallway and we walk toward the gym. I need some major reassurance after Jake's revelation.

"Hey, Ash. You okay, you look a little down," she says.

"I'm alright, I just want to get this stupid weekend over

with." I look down at my feet.

"Don't blame you. This is a good test for Andrew."

"What do you mean 'good test'?"

"If he really likes you, he won't do anything."

"But, what if he does?" I ask.

"Dump his ass."

This is a good test. Take that Jake, I'm in control and I'm testing Andrew. But, am I really?

Yellow streamers and balloons dangle from the ceiling. The band plays go, fight, win songs in the background. The excitement is palpable.

I spot Andrew sitting with the football team, laughing with Mark. Then, I spot Megan, hair up in ribbons swaying her body with her pom-poms smacking together to the rhythm of the band. All the cheerleaders are wearing a football player's jersey over their uniforms. It's the stupid secret player thing. The cheerleaders leave notes in the player's lockers, wear their jerseys, and toilet paper their houses. I spot Megan's number. Surprise, it's Andrew's. I'd love to shove her pom-poms up her plump posterior.

Lizzy reads my mind as she scans the cheerleaders. "Wouldn't you love to punch her?"

"You have no idea."

"Don't worry, I'll make sure she doesn't put one paw on him."

Thank God for Lizzy.

The Pep Rally is actually pretty fun. Lizzy and I spend most of the time mocking Megan. When the soccer team is called, we line up and do our cheer. The school makes a big deal out of our team because we're undefeated for the second year in a row. While I'm standing in line, Andrew looks so proud, staring at me the whole time. One of his teammates whispers something in his ear. They laugh and slap high five.

Chaos breaks out in the hallway as the gym clears after the Pep Rally ends. The football team yells testosterone filled chants. Andrew sprints up behind me and picks me up like a newlywed. I feel like a queen with her king. He deposits me by my locker, plants a kiss, and rejoins his teammates.

Take that mousy Megan.

I grab my stuff out of my locker, excited to play some serious soccer and forget about the stupid dance.

Sports are such a sweet escape. After two hours of mind-blowing, minus the Megan misery messing with my brain soccer, I swing my cleat-filled bag over my shoulder. Another close one against Cape Catholic. They almost got us, but with two minutes left, Kate sent a beautiful cross to Jillian who fired the ball right by the goalie and into the net, keeping our perfect record unscathed.

We're cheering and chanting on our way to the bus. Everyone's ear-to-ear smiles. What a win.

I snap back to reality and reach into my bag.

Fr: Andrew

Hope you won. Meet me at the beach at 7.

10/16/07   **5:05 p.m.**

Hugging the phone to my chest, I plop on the seat behind the bus driver, pout, and place my headphones into my ears hoping to drown out my roaring teammates who are planning on partying all weekend.

As soon as I get home, I jump into the shower, run some eyeliner across my eyes, squeeze into my skinny jeans, match them with a new tank, blow dry my hair straight, and grab Andrew's hoody in case the beach is chilly. Lizzy meets me at the corner, checks me over, adds some lip gloss to my pre-date prep and we're off. We practically sprint down the streets to meet Mark and Andrew.

Andrew looks effortlessly hot in his perfect butt-hugging jeans and another grey hoody over his thick chest. His dark tuft of hair, still wet from his shower, shines from the light rays of the setting sun. He greets me with a kiss and grabs my hand. We walk a couple steps to our spot in the dunes.

"Do you want to stop here?" he asks.

A gentle smile graces his lips as he looks down at me. I want to enjoy this moment and not be a pest, I can't help it, I'm not in the mood to spend the night kissing him, even though I know I'm getting really good at the kissing thing. It's kind of like pitching. The more you practice, the better you get.

"Not really. I'm too hyper." I scan the road. "Let's go to the playground."

"The playground?" Andrew looks at me like I'm speaking Japanese.

"Yeah, I'm in the mood to play," I say.

Andrew grins. "Okay." He shrugs his shoulders.

Not that kind of play, you pervert. That totally came out wrong.

"I'll race you," I say. I take off toward the playground across the street from the beach, but Andrew easily beats me by twenty feet. He's so quick. I wish I had his speed. If I did, colleges would be drooling to recruit me like they drool to recruit him.

Centered in the playground is a huge wooden jungle gym. Andrew sprints to the monkey bars and flips upside down on a bar. Big, hot, jock Andrew swinging upside down on the monkey bars. If only all of Sunray could see him now.

I plant a kiss on him hoping to reenact the Spiderman scene. He laughs so hard he let's go of the bars and tumbles to the ground. Then, he stands up and wraps his arms around my waist. He's going in for the kiss. Instead, I turn my head and point.

"Look, there's a basketball." Sitting by itself is a worn orange basketball behind the basketball net. "Let's play." I say

After stalling some more playing one-on-one, a sweaty Andrew plops down on the side of the court.

"What's wrong?" I ask.

"I'm exhausted, Ash. I have a big game tomorrow. I shouldn't be playing this much basketball the night before a game. If Coach saw me, he would flip."

"Don't go with Megan." I spout out before I can take it back, but Jake's words replay in my head like a bad song I can't shake. This is my last inning two out attempt to get him to go alone.

Andrew takes a deep breath. "We've been over this again and again, Ash. I promise, you're number one. She's just a friend. Anyway, I have fun with you. I like you." He gently touches his full lips on mine. His big arms envelop me as we lounge on a bench.

After what seems like mere minutes of talking and laughing about everything, I glance down at my watch. I should have been home fifteen minutes ago, but I don't want to leave Andrew.

"Andrew, I've gotta go." I shout, "See you Mark and Lizzy." Mark and Lizzy are too busy in the dunes sucking face to notice I'm leaving. Everyone is getting wrapped up in homecoming hoopla.

My cell phone vibrates in my back pocket. "Hey. Sorry. I'll be home in ten minutes. I know. I know. Bye."

"Parents?" Andrew asks.

"Yup." For a moment, I wonder if Megan has a ridiculously early ten-thirty curfew like me.

"I'll walk you home," he says.

"I'd like that." I still want him to remember me happy, instead of bugging him about Megan like a greenhead fly on a hot summer day.

I savor every block until we reach my front step. Usually, I dart into the house, avoiding the awkwardness of worrying about my parents watching us kiss. I turn to grab the doorknob and feel Andrew grab my other hand.

"Wait, Ash."

"What. Andrew. I'm sorry. This is so hard missing your game and everything. I don't even want to go to mine. There's this girl Christy…"

"Tell me about it," he says as he squats to sit on my front step then sprawls his legs.

"This girl, she hates me and I don't know why. Except, that I'm the other pitcher and she's pissed about it."

"Did you talk to her?" He asks.

"Yeah," I pause. "Not really."

"Why don't you talk to her?"

"It's not that simple."

"When I have a problem with a guy on the team, we talk or fight, then it's over. Why don't you try that?"

"It's different with girls. Girls are meaner and they don't let things go." I grin remembering me bugging him.

"Well, at least try to talk to her and let me know how it goes," he says.

Why didn't I talk to him about this before? I feel closer to Andrew right now than I do when we kiss.

"Thanks," I say.

He places his index finger gently in front of my lips. "It'll be okay this weekend." He looks at me. "You have nothing to worry about because I think I'm falling in love with you, Ashley."

Did I hear him right? I'm ditching him for softball and he loves me? I forget about everything and kiss the boy who stole my heart. I close my eyes and kiss the boy who makes me melt.

"Me too."

Bottom of the Third
October, Freshman Year

Fr: Andrew

Good luck 2day miss u

10/6/07   **8:21 a.m.**

My parents, Max, and I cruise into the complex an hour earlier than game time. This is so typical. We always arrive earlier than everyone, even the grounds people. My dad says this allows me an opportunity to get into my zone. I think it wastes precious sleep time. I can get into my so-called zone during the three-hour car ride.

My dad is super into softball. When I turned seven and announced I wanted to try pitching, he took it up as a second hobby, taking me to lessons, learning everything he could, and ordering tons of pitching books. Then, when I pitched my first game and threw so hard that my poor little playground friends wouldn't even enter the batter's box or talk to me for like a week after the game, my dad became obsessed. See, my dad loves sports. A local Sunray sports legend in his own right, any excuse to spend time playing or watching sports, he's there.

"Ashley," I mouth the words along with my father. "Why don't you sit in the dugout and work on getting into your zone?"

Max is in dreamland, so my parents stay in the car, which is perfect. Time to sneak away. I duck out of the car and snatch my bag out of the trunk.

The infield orange dirt matches the orange leaves on the trees that surround the fields. A crisp breeze is cool against my skin while the cloudless sky gives way to a warm autumn sun. I walk toward the dugout avoiding the chalk lines and flip open my phone.

Andrew's voicemail picks right up. I disconnect and text him instead.

To: Andrew

Miss u 2 good luck <3 me

10/6/07   **8:38 a.m.**

Then, I try Lizzy.

"Hello?" Lizzy says.

"Hey Liz, it's me."

"Aren't you at your game?" Lizzy asks.

"I'm here already. Call me after the dance, okay? I want to know every detail, like if Andrew touches Megan, how many times they dance, and if he," I pause, "does it with her in the corner of the dance or something."

"Oh my God, Ashley, did you get hit in the head with a softball or something? He doesn't care about that slut."

"Still, this is a test. I want to know if he passes or fails." Doesn't she remember her test advice?

"Oh, yeah, the test. No problem. Did you have fun with Andrew last night? When Mark and I left, we couldn't find you guys anywhere?"

"You were busy. Anyway, Andrew told me he was falling for me."

"What? And you're worried about a skank? Come on, Ash, get real."

"I guess you're right. It's just hard when he has Megan throwing herself at him and other girls just lining up, waiting to. Especially when, I'm like miles away at this dumb-ass tournament."

"Ashley, breathe. I told you, I'll watch Andrew," Lizzy reminds me.

"I know, Liz. I just think I'm starting to really have strong feelings for him. I mean at this point if he did mess around with Megan, I'd be crushed."

"Somebody's falling in love." Lizzy chants, "Ashley loves Andrew…."

Hearing this out loud makes my stomach feel weird.

"Shut up. I have to go."

"Good luck. I'll call you after the dance. Hey, have fun. You're not married… yet."

"Whatever. Call me, later."

I snap my phone shut and I'm left feeling bare, like my heart is out there for the world to see. At first, Andrew was just this hottie. I thought he would like date me twice, we'd have fun, and then he'd take off. Then, I'd go back to obsessing about sports. I almost skipped this tournament to go to a dance with Andrew. Who am I? Ashley before Andrew would have never done something like that.

I relax back against the cold hard bench and spot Amy, Stephanie, and Christy giggling as they walk collectively toward me. My stomach turns inside out. I take a deep breath, stand up, and tuck my shirt into my shorts. Why do I have no problem pitching in front of fans, but I can't handle a little heart to heart with Christy?

"Hi," I squeak.

They ignore me as they continue their Christy led conversation outside the dugout.

This has got to stop. I've had enough. If I'm going to stay on the Crush, then I have to talk to Christy one on one just like Andrew said. I pull my shoulders back ready for Christy combat. I look right into her angry aqua eyes.

"Christy, can I talk to you for a minute?" I ask.

She glances at Stephanie, then Amy. "I'm surprised to see

you here, Ash. I was sure you'd be at the dance with Andrew. I mean, who lets their boyfriend go to a dance with another girl? Especially someone as hot as Megan?"

Stephanie and Amy share identical giggles.

Her words slash through me. For a moment, I contemplate turning around and revisiting my seat on the bench, but I'm sick of this, sick of her shit.

"Can we talk over here?" I say pointing toward left field.

"Sure." She drops her bag and turns around.

Stephanie and Amy are left open-mouthed. Their eyes burn the back of my head as I follow Christy to left field away from her adoring fans.

With my index nail between my teeth, I stare at my damp cleats as they shuffle through the grass. I try to remember the re-hearsed lines I invented during the car ride here. But, I'm drawing a blank. Instead, I hug my chest.

"What?" Christy rests her arms on her hips as she sways her body to the right like she's balancing a baby on her hip.

"I just want to know what your problem is with me," I say.

"I don't know what you're talking about, Ashley."

"You've been pretty mean to me since my first day. What did I ever do to you?" I puff my chest and take a deep breath.

"You're imagining things. Lighten up."

"Of the five words you've managed to say to me, it's always been mean. Like, I shouldn't be on a sixteen and under team and

Coach isn't going to play me. You've never given me a chance." I'm on a roll. "What the hell did I ever do to you?"

Okay, why is she grinning?

"Let me tell you something. As much as you want it to be, it's not always about you, Ashley Clarke. Get over yourself. All we ever hear is, 'I miss my boyfriend,' or, 'I was up late talking to Andrew.' It's about the team, Ash." With that, she completes a half-circle and hauls her big ass toward the dugout.

I'm left standing in left field staring at where the infield dirt meets the green grass. New to this cutthroat softball world of sixteen and under, I begin to wish I was getting ready for the football game, instead of this tournament. Christy did have one tiny point. I do spend a lot of time thinking about Andrew and it does distract me from the team at times. But, she hated me before she even knew me. I spin around in the hopes of finding a hideout as far away from Christy and her cronies as humanly possible.

After at least twenty minutes of pretending to use the bathroom, I'm afraid I'm going to miss the start, so I drag myself toward the field at a snail's pace.

"Ashley."

Like a patient with post-traumatic stress disorder, I frantically whip my head around and spot Kate behind me.

"Hi, Kate." I breathe a sigh of relief.

"Do you feel awful missing homecoming?" Kate asks.

"Truth, yeah. But, I'll get over it. Softball is more important to me right now." I fib.

"Yeah, I wish I could go, but I'd rather be here, too." She smiles.

I'd love to be more like her. No worries. Everyone loves her. No boyfriend.

"So, are you ready for today?" she asks as the sun exposes her nose freckles. Her pale blond hair is wrapped in two French braids on each side of her head.

"Yup. I'm ready. I hope I pitch."

"It's a long tournament. You'll get time."

Familiar flutters loom in my belly once again as I spot Christy, Amy, and Stephanie stretching together on the outfield grass.

"Want to warm-up?" Kate asks.

"Sure." I grab a ball from the bucket.

"Hi, Ashley," Coach D looks up from under her orange visor as she balances the scorebook on her lap. I take a quick peek at the lineup.

"Hi, Coach," I answer. I can't quite spot my name. I don't blame her after the last start.

Kate and I locate a spot to throw in left field. I try not to, but I glance over at Christy, Amy, and Stephanie. Amy looks at me and rolls her eyes.

"Hi, Kate. Ready for today?" Christy asks ignoring my existence.

"Hi, Christy," Kate smiles.

Whatever. Now I regret saying anything to Christy. She'll never like me. If I want to play on the Crush, I have to learn to deal with girls like her or quit.

After a couple of tosses with Kate, Coach calls us together for a huddle.

"Christy, Ashley, go warm up together. Emily, get your equipment on for throw downs. You're starting this one, Christy." Coach tosses the brand new yellow ball at Christy. Christy shoots a look my way that says, you're such a loser.

Christy walks ahead of me, finds a spot, and tosses me the ball. We warm up in silence. I try to concentrate on perfecting my rise ball. This is the last tournament of the fall season. After this weekend, I don't have to deal with Christy until winter practices begin.

After warm-ups, Coach calls us together for a quick talk. The team is dragging. Coach works her magic and pumps us up. Afterwards, I find a spot at the far end of the bench. I settle in, get comfortable, and prepare to watch Christy take the mound.

After five quick innings, I stand up and check the bench for an imprint of my butt. There has to be a permanent mark. The team huddles around Christy to congratulate her on her one-hitter. I'm hoping I'll get my chance next game to prove myself again.

Looking down at my cleats and clean uniform, I ease over

Christy's way. "Nice win," I say.

She pretends she doesn't hear me and saunters past me into the dugout.

Behind her, Stephanie's eyes are as big as walnuts.

"You're starting next game, Ashley." Coach snaps me out of my trance. "The Blue Devils are tough. Their number four hitter likes them inside. We know you can shut them down."

"I'm ready, Coach," I say. I'm so ready. I sat through five innings and watched Christy pitch a one-hitter against a nothing team. I'll show everyone what I've got.

I swing my bag onto my shoulder. An urge to grab my phone takes me over, but I fight it and instead turn my thoughts toward the next game. My game. I spot the field and sprint toward it.

It's only the bottom of the first inning of the second game and we're already up by four runs. I jog to the pitcher's mound feeling good. Bending down, I snatch the game ball.

After my three-pitch warm-up, I receive the ball from Kate. The Blue Devil's first batter digs in. Emily gives the sign. I wind up and release my drop ball. It sails straight, and then bottoms out. The batter's eyes widen, but the pitch dips in time.

"Strike."

Emily tosses the ball back to me. I hollow out the mound to make it more comfortable. Another sign; rise ball. Perfect. I wind up, spin my wrist, and release. It tails up, throwing the batter off balance. She swings again and misses.

"Strike."

The batter tunnels the box once again with one foot outside the white line. She faces third base. Emily gives me a change-up sign. Nice call.

I wind up and release the change. The batter begins her swing days before the pitch. She attempts to hold back. Too late.

"Strike."

One down, two to go. Emily whips the ball to Kate. The infielders toss the ball around. Maggie receives the ball last and jogs it to me. We slap hands.

With ease, I strike out the side.

As we trot toward the dugout, I'm tempted to smile at Christy, but instead I stand up to cheer for my teammates.

First up, Kate takes a few practice swings, then enters the batter's box. She cracks a perfect, down-the-middle line drive. Maggie digs in next. She walks, moving Kate to second. I grab my bat and walk toward the batter's circle.

Emily also walks on four pitches. Bases loaded. No outs.

I burrow my right cleat into the orange dirt. I turn to Coach D. She gives me her signs. Green light. I turn to face the pitcher. She nods and winds up. The yellow ball whizzes inside, my sweet spot.

Smack! The ball sails into left field. Kate, Maggie, and Emily take off. Our first base coach points to second. I round first, then second, and look up at Coach D who's waving me to third. As I round second, her arms are in the air, palms facing my way. I brake at third. A stand-up triple with three RBI's. Coach D slaps me a high five. The entire team is on their feet, cheering.

Six innings later, I'm floating after pitching a two-hitter with twelve strikeouts and no walks. I'd rather have pitched a one-hitter or even better, a no-hitter.

In the dugout, I pull off my slider and push down my socks. Dirt clouds puff off my socks. The best thing about an orange uniform is it hides the dirt.

As I reach for my slides, my cell phone tumbles out of my bag. I catch it before it hits the concrete. I almost forgot about Andrew, the dance, and Megan. I check the time. Two hours and counting until Megan picks up Andrew for the dance. My heart sinks. I think about calling Andrew and telling him about the win and my talk with Christy, but I'm afraid it will make me feel even worse.

"Why the long face, Ashley? Didn't Andrew call you? Or is he too busy screwing Megan?" Christy stands scowling in front of me.

Ouch. Of course, Stephanie and Amy are right behind her. I decide to strike back.

"Do you really think that bothers me. Coming from you?" I say.

"Here we go again, it's always about Ashley. Me, me, me." Christy rolls her eyes for the audience.

I stand up. "You're just pissed because I'm good enough to play for this team. Good as you and I'm two years younger. How's that make you feel, Chris? I guess that's why you are so nasty to me. Because I'm better than you."

I grab my bag and stomp out of the opening in the dugout holding my head high. I walk directly to my parent's car without turning back. I feel good leaving Christy in the dirt.

"What do you want to do for dinner, Ashley?" my dad asks me on our trip back to the hotel.

I'm sure I didn't score points with my teammates after my Christy blowout, but I still secretly hope I hang out with the team tonight. It would distract me from the dance. "I don't care, dad." I answer.

"What's the team doing?"

"I don't know. Let me call Kate." I pull out my phone.

"I want McDonalds," my brother chants.

Kate's voicemail picks up. "Hey Kate, it's Ashley. Let me know what the team is doing for dinner. Give me a call."

At the hotel, I jump into the shower. The steamy water feels great against my back, instantly loosening my shoulders. My anxiety about Andrew and the dance collect in the water on my back, slide down the drain, and wash away. After tonight, the season's over. I'll have Andrew all to myself again.

I blow-dry my hair straight and slap on some make-up. Lizzy would be so disappointed, spending less than five minutes on my face. I flip open my phone. No messages. That's odd that Kate never called me back. I call her again, but her voicemail picks up. I'm sure she'll call me back soon.

"Ready to go?" I ask my mom. Max is jumping like a monkey on the bed. "Where's dad?"

"He went to find some of the parents to see where everyone is going tonight."

Just then, my dad opens the hotel door.

"No luck," he says. "I can't seem to find anyone."

"I'll try Kate again," I say.

I grab my phone from the table, flip it open again and dial Kate.

She answers after the second ring.

"Hey Kate. It's Ashley. Where is everyone going for dinner?"

She pauses. "I got your message, but I was about to call you back when Christy said you told her you were really tired and you were going right to bed. We're about to get on a Haunted Hayride. Sorry, Ashley."

I take a deep breath. "It's not your fault Kate." I contemplate telling Kate about Christy's lie, but then I'd be a loser like her.

Christy would just deny it anyway.

"See you tomorrow, Ashley. If we do anything else, I'll call you."

"Thanks, Kate." I close my phone.

"So, where is everyone?" my dad asks.

"They're on a Haunted Hayride." I look down at my phone.

"Oh." I glance up to see my mom look at dad then at her hands. She begins to play with her rings.

"You know what, I heard there is a really nice Italian place up the road."

"Food!" Max shouts. He jumps higher and faster.

"What do you think, Ash?" She looks at me out of the corner of her eye and frowns. She knows how girls are. My dad has no clue. My mom hates Italian food because of the high carb content. Italian is my favorite. I appreciate my mom's gesture. After the day I've had, I'd rather flop on the bed and watch a sappy Lifetime movie while spooning ice cream, than go anywhere.

"I'm not feeling real good. I think I'll stay back."

"What are you going to eat? Come on, Ashley," my mom pleads.

"Really, I'm not that hungry."

"We'll have fun, Ash," my dad adds.

"Let's go. She doesn't want to go." Max says, pulling my mom's arm toward the door.

"No, really. I'm okay. I just want to relax." I pause. "And

focus on my games tomorrow. You know, get into my zone."

My dad grins. "If you insist. We'll call from the restaurant so you can give us your order. Then, we'll drop it off."

"Okay," I say. 'Getting into the zone' always works.

Max drags my mom out the door. My dad follows behind. Just before he closes the door, he says, "Bye, Sweetheart."

I sprawl across the bed, grab for the remote and eye the fridge. I bet there are some goodies in there, so I slide from my spot and open the fridge door. Yum. I grab a Coke from the fridge and a Hershey bar and Twizzlers from the basket above then snuggle back up under the sheets.

I channel surf looking for Lifetime.

An hour later, my head is buzzing from the caffeine and I'm depressed because everything about the stupid Lifetime movie reminds me of Andrew. The guy who stalks his girlfriend has the same color hair as Andrew. The guy who impregnates his wife's sister has the same dimples as Andrew. I wonder if Andrew has had sex, yet. We just kiss. Nothing else and he never tries anything else.

The glaring red numbers on the clock read eight o'clock. They must be at the dance by now.

My boyfriend is at a dance with a skank. My team hates me. Christy is making my life on the Crush miserable. I shake my head trying to force thoughts of Megan and Andrew kissing, holding each other, dancing, and having a blast out of my mind.

I grab my phone and text Lizzy.

To: Lizzy

How's dance?

10/6/07   **8:09 p.m.**

I wait and wait. Now the Lifetime woman is in serious dog poop. She's pregnant with her sister's husband's baby. Way too confusing. My ring tone. Andrew?

"Hello?"

"Hey, Ashley, how are you doing?" my mom says.

"I'm fine mom." I answer disappointed.

"Are you sure?" she asks. "You sound depressed. Is it the new team? Is it Andrew? You can tell me, Boo."

"Mom, I'm fine," I lie.

"Do you want to order something? We'll bring it home."

"Um. Okay, how about chicken parm?" I ask.

"Okay, we'll bring it home in about a half hour. Call us if you need anything."

I flip the phone closed. My stomach growls. I flip the phone back open and text Andrew.

To: Andrew

Miss you.

10/6/07   **8:58 p.m.**

Before I press send, I wonder if I sound like a total loser. I want him to feel the same way I do right now. I could be out with some hot guy who thinks I'm the best pitcher ever for all he knows, not sitting on a bed surrounded by empty candy wrappers watching Lifetime movies. I delete the message. Instead, I channel surf for sports or something that doesn't remind me of Andrew.

Knots fill my stomach worse than when I'm facing a big game. I'm done. I've wasted too much time worrying about this. I shut my phone off only to turn it on again. I feel like I'm playing tug-of-war with normal Ashley and psycho in love with Andrew Ashley. What happened to me? I rest my head on the pillow, shut my phone off, and wait for my dinner.

I wake up face to face with Max's open mouth. His rotten morning breath, a combination of garlic and old cheese, is filling my nostrils. He seriously needs to learn how to brush better. I turn my back to him and stare at the butt-ugly, thick, paisley hotel curtains. In bold red numbers the clock reads six thirty-five. My parents' bed is empty. They're probably out for a morning jog or coffee.

My first game is in two-and-a-half hours. My phone is staring at me from across the room, taunting my self-control. I reach for it. Turning it on, I wipe the sleep out of my eyes.

A few seconds later, my phone beeps. Three text messages.

My heart races.

Two from Lizzy and one from Andrew.

Fr: Lizzy

Dance waz fun miss u Andrew waz perfect never even danced w/

Meg

10/7/07   **12:02 a.m.**

The hundred pound weight resting on my shoulders lifts.

Fr: Lizzy

He did leave w/ her in group. But no big deal. Don't want u 2

worry see u tom

10/7/07   **12:07 a.m.**

It's back. What do you mean, no big deal? It's a big freakin'

deal. Did they have sex? Is that why they left together? Did Megan

do her lipstick trick? My alter ego, Andrew's Ashley, is back with a

vengeance. I check the one from Andrew for clues.

Fr: Andrew

Miss u wish u were here see u tom

10/7/07   **1:49 a.m.**

One o'clock in the morning. I've been so freaked out about

the dance. I didn't even bother to think about after-parties or after

stuff. Totally one hundred percent worse. So, what did he do be-

tween eleven and one o'clock in the morning? My heart sinks.

Max kicks my side. I shut the phone off again. My thoughts

are swirling. Should I continue to date Andrew and fall deeper in love with him? But, then my softball suffers big time. Or, should I dump him and suffer some serious heartbreak? At least, then I can concentrate solely on softball. But when I think of Andrew dating someone else, I seethe. And what the hell would I do with myself? Become some softball chick that doesn't do anything but play ball? Loser.

I take a deep breath and get dressed. I have a superstitious routine, underwear first, then socks, then shirt, then sliding shorts, then uniform shorts, and finally, I pull up my socks. Before I leave, I fix my hair. Yesterday, I wore a ponytail with an orange and yellow ribbon. Today, same ponytail since I had a great game yesterday.

"You ready yet?" my dad asks. "I was downstairs with some of the parents from the Wildcats, the team you're playing today. They said they have one heck of a pitcher. So, if you're starting, this should be one heck of a pitcher's duel."

I roll my eyes and grab Andrew's grey hoody from the chair. Only my dad would find parents from the other team to scout at six in the morning. My mom's faint giggles fill the room as she gently shakes Max.

During the car ride to the field, I breathe in the scent of Andrew that lingers on the sweatshirt.

"Thinking about the game, Ash? I'm really proud of your dedication this weekend. You've really been in your zone," my dad shouts over Grateful Dead tunes.

If only he knew what I'm thinking about. My mom turns around and smiles at me.

"Good luck," my mom, says as we pull into the same parking space as yesterday. Did I mention Dad is superstitious too?

"Goo Luch," Max squirts out in between bits of his Pop Tart.

I sigh and look at my watch. Exactly one hour early again. I lug myself out of the car, grab my bag, and walk toward the empty dugout.

Christy, Stephanie, and Amy arrive about five minutes later. Just like yesterday, I grin, say hello, and continue feeling ignored. I contemplate calling Christy on the lie yesterday, but she'll remind me how I think life is all about me. I'm not going to win with her.

I spin a softball into my glove as I wait for Kate to show up, making a mental note to try to collect more friends today.

"Hi Ashley, we missed you last night," Maggie arrives next.

I pause thinking about what I should say, but I decide against my first instinct, which is to berate Christy. Instead, I go for the gentler, make friends with me approach. "Yeah, sorry I missed it."

"Want to have a catch?" she asks.

"Sure." I answer quicker than a swing.

I grab a ball and line up next to Christy.

"I'm done," Christy declares as she stares at me. Her cronies follow her like celebrity bodyguards.

Whatever, it gives me a chance to really get to know Maggie without crazy Christy distractions.

Maggie and I toss the ball back and forth and cover everything from Andrew to Lizzy to my old team. After I'm done, Maggie eyes are huge.

"I knew you and Andrew were dating, but I can't believe you're playing as well as you are with all that stuff on your mind," Maggie says. Her ponytail of bright dyed red and black hair sprouts out the top of her visor. Maggie's legs stretch for miles.

We begin our team warm-ups. Christy and I stroll to our spot. Last night during my Lifetime marathon, I made the decision to ignore Christy. I'm better off keeping my mouth shut.

Neither Christy or I know who's starting today, and both games are equally important. The first one gets us into the finals or consolations. But, the final game could be the championship game.

After the warm-up, Coach D calls us together in right field. We gather on the grass. I begin to pull at the blades one by one, the soft green strands slipping through my fingers. I look up at Coach, squinting to avoid the glare of the bright October sun, which feels like a warm blanket on a chilly morning.

"Okay, this is it," she begins. "Our game, our tournament. Christy and Ashley you're going to work together today. While, Christy is pitching, Ashley, you'll be keeping notes on batters. And vice versa. I want you both working together and ready to go in at anytime."

Christy's aqua eyes squint. She makes a puke face. I look back at the blades. So much for my ignoring Christy plan.

Coach continues her speech. "Ashley, you're starting." Butterflies flutter.

After her speech, we cheer. I jog to the mound and grab the unscathed yellow ball. Then, I dig in the mound. Sports sweet escape in its purest form. The dance is over. No more worries.

Two batters down after throwing only six pitches and I'm in a rhythm. The third batter glances at her coach and digs in. I take my sign from Emily. Rise ball. I wind up and release. It doesn't rise. The batter cracks the ball to left field. Stephanie is right there for the catch. One, two, three, and we're out of the inning.

Out of the corner of my eye, I spy my parents sitting in their usual lounge chairs. Who is that hot guy talking to my dad? Could it be? And the gorgeous girl next to him with the LaSalle soccer tee. Is that her?

Standing next to my dad in mesh shorts and a Sunray Beach football tee is Andrew. Next to him is Chloe, Andrew's older sister. They are both staring at me.

"Are you okay?" Maggie asks.

I point to Andrew. "That's him."

"Awwww. He drove all the way to watch you play. How sweet."

I smile. He is amazing. I'm freaking out inside. He drove three hours, yes three hours, to see me play. I resist the urge to run to him and jump into his arms.

As I wait for my turn to bat, I can't help but to continue to gawk at Andrew. He's sitting on the bleachers while Max hangs on his back. Max's arms are draped around Andrew's neck. Max is hysterical while Andrew wrestles with him. Chloe is sitting next to Andrew, talking to my mom. I forget about the texts, asking him where he was, the dance. He's here. He's here to see me play.

Speaking of his sister, Chloe. I am Chloe's official sixth grade stalker. Back in sixth grade, my dad would drag me to high school games. Every game, my eyes were glued to Chloe.

Back then, she was a soccer and softball legend at Sunray. During her senior year, she landed a full ride to LaSalle University in Philadelphia. I haven't really had a chance to meet her in person since LaSalle's soccer season started right when I met Andrew, so I'm equally excited to finally get a chance to talk with her.

I clearly remember Chloe. The way she wore her shorts, tucked her shirt, even the glove she used. I studied her and wanted to be her. She wore her light brown hair high in a ponytail with a thin headband holding her fly aways. I wore mine the same way that year.

"Ashley, you're up," Kate yells.

I snap out of my Chloe trance and grab my bat from the fence. I concentrate on the pitcher's wind-up and study her pitch selection. Emily is up with a full count. I bet the pitcher will throw a change-up, I think to myself.

"Watch the change," I yell to Emily.

Sure enough, a knee-buckling change launches out of the pitcher's hand. Emily holds back and unloads on the pitch. The ball sails to deep left field. The runners advance and we're up 1-0.

It's weird, sort-of paranormal. I've always been able to guess pitches. Sure, I can usually tell by the grip or the way the pitcher releases the ball. But, I have this weird sixth sense about it.

Before I trudge up to bat, I check to make sure my shirt is perfectly tucked in and my shorts are sitting on my hips just right. I hear Andrew cheering for me. I grin.

I'm flipping out. Andrew's here. Thump. I totally miss the bat lying on the grass in front of the batter's box. My outstretched hands stop the fall. But, I still land on all fours as I launch my bat toward the umpire.

Everyone is silent, except for Christy's cackles. Slowly, I stand up and peek a glance at Andrew. His hand is in front of his mouth. In fact, pretty much everyone's hands are in front of their mouths. Are they scared I'm hurt or are they stopping themselves from cracking up? I wipe the grass patches from my knees and batting gloves. Finally, I adjust my slider. My cheeks are flaming.

Gingerly, I step to the side of the batter's box for signs from Coach D. Emily's at first. Maggie's at third. Coach gives me the "take a pitch" sign to advance Emily to second. With two outs, I wonder if the catcher will throw. She's got a strong arm.

I dig in. The pitcher winds up. I fake a bunt. Emily takes off. The catcher stands up and fires the ball to second.

The umpire punches the air, "Out!"

Emily stands up and dusts off. I hang my head and jog into the dugout and grab my glove.

I mow down three in a row. I'm flying high after a good night's rest and of course, my excitement to perform for Andrew.

I grab my bat again. First up. I take a few swings. Coach D stands next to me.

"Take a look at her first pitch. She loves to get that first strike," she says.

Coach D strolls to her square. I step into the batter's box.

The pitcher winds up. I swing ahead of the ball and barely make contact. The ball dribbles in front of the batter's box. I drop the bat and take a step, but my legs feel heavy and the dirt feels like mud.

I tumble two steps out of the batters box. I watch the pitcher lazily grab the ball and easily toss it to first base. I hoist myself up and sprint toward first. I'm a total klutz. I wipe my shorts, and meander to the dugout. The dugout is silent. My teammates steal glances at each other and cover their mouths. I'm sure they all know Andrew is here. It's bad enough to fall once, but twice. I sit at the end of the bench to survey the damage to my knees. Blood, grass, and dirt stain the top of my socks.

"You okay?" I didn't realize it, but I sat smack next to Amy.

"Yeah, thanks." Then, I remember, I'm supposed to be working with Christy on pitches. I've been so preoccupied with Andrew and Chloe. I look down at her with the notebook. After I wipe my knee with some first aid ointment and slap on some band-aids, I get up and walk toward Christy.

I attempt again. "What are you seeing so far? What's my pitch count?"

Silence.

"Look, Christy, this is about the team, not me and you. We have to get along at least on the field."

Nothing. She stares at the field and slides the notebook toward me. I look at her notes. Okay, a baby step, but still a step.

The game is pretty uneventful after my fall or shall I say falls. I shut down the opposing team through four innings, then, Christy takes the mound and holds them through the last three.

After we slap hands, I'm equally excited about talking with Chloe and hugging Andrew, than I am about the finals. I grab my bag and sprint toward Andrew.

My cheeks hurt I'm smiling so wide.

"Andrew, I'm so glad you're here," I say as I resist the urge to hug him tight, but I'm embarrassed in front of my parents.

"I can see that. What happened in the batter's box?"

"There was something wrong with my cleats," I lie.

"Ashley, this is my sister, Chloe."

"Hi. I'm so excited you're here. It's so nice to meet you Chloe. You are such a great athlete. I kept telling Andrew I couldn't wait to meet you. Oh my God, how's LaSalle?" I ramble.

She looks at me and moves her oversized shades on top of her head.

"Hi, Ashley. It's nice to meet you too," she says extending her hand.

I shake it. Then, I look at Andrew. Tingles run up and down my spine.

"Are you okay?" he asks as he looks down at maroon stained orange striped white socks.

"Yeah, I'm alright now."

He smiles.

"How was your game?" I ask Andrew.

"Great. We won by a touchdown. I have the tape. I want you to watch it with me sometime this week. Wait, until you see my touchdown pass. It was executed perfectly." He drones on and on.

When I hear a pause, I ask, "How was the dance?" Chloe is walking a little ahead of us toward the snack stand.

"Okay. I danced, then we hung out, and I went home."

"What did you do afterwards?" I ask.

"We hung out at Scott's house for a bit. Then I went home. I missed you."

Scott. Scott is the biggest party animal at Sunray. He's the center on the football team. Scott's parents' own arcades up and down the coast. His parties are crazy. Or so I've heard. I'm always playing softball. So, I've never actually made it to one. More thoughts creep into my head. I push them out with all my might. He's here. But, I can't resist one more.

"How did Megan look?"

"Ashley, I didn't even notice. I was busy thinking about you."

"Yeah, right," I giggle. "Good one."

"No, I'm serious. Stop, Ash. The stupid dance is over and nothing happened. Come on, can you please just drop it? Anyway, I'm here."

"Great game, Ash. I remember when you were pitching in Cape Town Little League. You are one hell of a pitcher," Chloe interrupts.

Chloe's hair is amazing. It's honey colored and pulled in a high ponytail, with side sweeping bangs.

"Thanks."

"I told you Ashley's a great pitcher," Andrew says.

"Yeah, you've been telling me a lot about Ashley." Chloe grins and pinches Andrew's dimple. Andrew smacks her hand away. I giggle. Tough jock Andrew ain't so tough around his big sis.

"Your next game is over there," my dad interrupts us as he points to the field by the kiddy park.

"Okay, I'll head that way in a sec," I say.

"Nice to see you again, Chloe. Thanks for coming," my dad shakes Andrew and Chloe's hands and heads toward the field with his chair rolled up like a giant tootsie roll hanging over his shoulder.

"Are you guys hungry?" Andrew asks Chloe and I.

"I am," Chloe answers.

"Let's get some grub."

We walk to the snack stand. My teammates are shoved on two picnic benches devouring an enormous amount of pizza, hot-dogs, and juice. Coach isn't that strict about food, but she absolutely bans soda. If she catches you with it, it's one lap for the whole team. Of course, Christy pushed the issue a couple of weeks ago and we ran for it.

I order the same as Chloe. I figure whatever she's eating works. As always, Andrew orders a ton of food.

We find a deserted picnic bench. Being with Andrew and his sister is really starting to make me feel like I'm part of his life, and I'm lovin' every moment.

"So, where do you want to go to college?" Chloe asks me while popping chips into her mouth.

"Chlo, she's only a freshman," Andrew says.

"Whatever." Chloe slaps the air. "You knew since you were eight, you wanted to go to Notre Dame."

"I guess, I'll go with whoever will take me," I interrupt.

"Take you?" Chloe answers. "You're good, Ash. A college is

lucky to have you."

I'm staring at Chloe's caramel highlights. I should really think of highlighting my own hair.

"How's soccer?" I ask her.

I chomp away listening to Chloe talk about soccer. I don't want this meal to end ever.

We're still lazing over our wrapper and cups, when I hear my teammates shouting, "One, two, three,"

"I have to go," I say.

"I'll get your trash," Andrew says. He pecks me on the cheek as I get up from the bench.

"Awwww," I hear Chloe say. "My little bro. Driving three hours for a girl. He even cleans up after her, too. So cute."

I grin. With softballs tossing around in my stomach, I swing my bag over my shoulder and sprint back to another field, another game, another diamond, and another interrupted chance to be with Andrew.

Within seconds, I squeeze in between Maggie and Kate.

"He is smoking hot," Maggie says to me as I bend over.

I smile.

"He sure is. Didn't he take some hot cheerleader to the dance yesterday?" Christy announces to the team.

"Do you even have a boyfriend?" I spurt out before I can bring the words back.

Christy's face turns into a cherry.

"If you only knew," she says.

Maggie glances my way. I swear I catch a grin.

Christy gets the start this time. Coach D wants me to warm-up, ready for the final innings. I'm beat, but excited to play again in front of Andrew and Chloe.

For two innings I sit on the bench and observe with my notebook and pen. After the third inning, it's still zero to zero. Coach turns to me. You're going in next inning. I smile and scan the field for Andrew. He's gone.

I jump. Andrew's face is in front of mine separated by the dugout fence.

"I have to leave. Chloe has practice early tomorrow morning and she has to get back to school," he says to me. I feel like I'm in a jail cell. I can't touch or kiss Andrew goodbye. I'm stuck in this softball slammer.

"Thanks for coming," I say.

"Call me and let me know how you do," he says.

I watch him turn around and walk away before I can show Chloe and Andrew what I'm really made out of at the plate.

I grab Emily for a quick warm-up before I take the mound, but I find myself staring out in space.

"You okay?" Emily asks me as I launch the third pitch over her head.

"Yeah, I guess," I say.

"That boy Andrew really gets under your skin," she says.

"No, I think I'm just worn out," I deny.

I shake my head hoping Andrew will magically pop out.

The team takes the field. Christy stays parked on the bench, where her nasty ass belongs.

I jog onto the mound.

Zero to zero, top of the fourth. While waiting for my turn to pitch, I studied their batters. I'm ready. I know what they have and I know what to expect.

Number two digs in. First batter in the lineup. Slaps or bunts every time. Emily knows her too. She sets up high and tight. I throw my screwball. Bong. Number two attempts a bunt, but it pops up right to Stephanie at third. One out.

Number fifteen digs in and takes signs from her coach. This one has some power, but likes to slap. She's speedy. I turn around and signal to Kate who pulls in the infield.

Emily gives me a sign. Rise ball. Good call. I wind up, but instead of rise, it stays straight down the middle. I swear I see saliva dripping from number fifteen's mouth as she swings and pounds the ball down the third base line. Stephanie is too close, and the ball sails into shallow left field. Number fifteen easily slides into second for a double before Amy even has time to throw in the ball.

One out, one girl on second. The last thing I want to do right now is blow the tie.

Number seven digs in. I look at Christy. I can't remember what I wrote for this one. Christy stares at me, expressionless. She knows why I'm looking at her.

I put my trust in Emily for this one. She sets up outside low. I wind up and hit the target. Strike one.

Next pitch. Emily sets up for a drop. I wind up. Number seven nails the pitch before it drops. Right by me and up the middle. Speedy on second rounds third and scores.

Emily calls time out. "No problem, Ash. Let's get out of this inning. The next batter is the fourth batter. We'll stay away from her and go after number five."

We slap gloves. I turn around to hollow out the mound and re-coupe. I'm back to Andrew's Ashley again. Andrew's Ashley equals shitty softball. One Andrew sighting and I'm mush.

I deep breathe, wind up, and release. Tension evaporates and I'm in a rhythm again. Six pitches later, we're out of the inning.

Jogging into the dugout, I spy Christy still clad with that simple smile. I know she's thinking if Coach kept her in, we would be winning. I think about saying something about her lack of help on the bench, but I decide against it. I'm determined to win this game. Even if I have to do it all by myself at the plate.

After three batters, we're on the field again. Three more batters, ten pitches, and three more strikeouts. I jog back to the dugout and grab my bat. I'm up first this time.

I watch the warm-up and take some practice swings. Coach is beside me observing the pitcher.

"Watch her rise. Move up in the box. Be ready for the bunt

sign. First swing green light," she says.

I adjust my slider and dig into the box. Homerun, I think to myself.

First pitch. Curveball, I see it before she even releases the ball. I lay-off.

I step out of the box and look down at Coach. She gives me the bunt sign. We're down one to nothing and I get the freakin' bunt sign. I know I can slam this pitcher.

I dig into the box. The pitcher releases a fastball, I swing. The ball sails to left field. The left fielder makes the easy catch by the fence. I jog into the dugout with my head down.

Two more batters and we're back on the field once again. Our bats are colder than the Delaware Bay in January.

"Christy, take the mound. Ashley take a break. While you're resting review the signs," Coach says.

Christy grabs her glove and jogs to the mound. Once again, I find my spot on the far end of the bench and pick up the notebook, but Coach isn't done with me.

"You might have been able to pull that junk on fourteen and under, but I have girls ready and willing to take your place at anytime, Ashley. If I give you a sign, you listen. Don't ever play Coach with me again," she says then turns around and returns to the field.

She's right. But, I never did anything like that before. I've never even been yelled at by a coach. I desperately wanted to get the run back to show Christy I'm better. But, all I did was give Christy another opportunity to show me up.

A chilly wind cuts through my skin. I grab Andrew's sweatshirt out of my bag and pull it over my head.

Top of the seventh, Christy takes the mound and lets up two more earned runs.

Bottom of the seventh, Maggie gets on with one out. Kate drives her home with a line drive double to center field. Christy hits a ground ball, which moves Kate to third. Power hitter Amy gets up and launches one to right field to bring Kate home. Stephanie's up with two outs and the tying run on first. We're all on our feet. She works a full count. The pitcher winds up for the pitch. The field is silent. The pitch sails in, Stephanie swings. She misses the perfect change-up by a mile. We lose by one run.

The other team is screaming and celebrating at home plate. We collect our tiny second place trophies and pack up. So close. A bittersweet ending to a bittersweet fall season. Well, at least I can rest assured I won't be missing anything until the spring. Now that I'm thinking about skipping the winter basketball season.

Top of the Fourth
November, Freshman Year

"Sweetheart, I heard you're quite the athlete. Are you excited about basketball?" Andrew's mom's eyes are the same tan color and massive size as Andrew's. She sits across from me in Andrew's immaculate dining room decorated for Turkey Day. About twenty of Andrew's relatives surround me, eyes glued on me, Andrew's girlfriend. I'm chomping on what's left of my nail.

"Uh. Yeah, I guess," I say. Not exactly the way I want to break my news. "Could you please pass the potatoes," I ask Chloe, trying to switch subjects.

The table cover is light cream and feels like silk, way too nice to eat off of. Instead of the table, it should be on someone's bed. Andrew's mom concocted this beautiful spread complete with real silver and china. I'm desperately tying to remember my manners. Even placing the matching beige silky cloth napkin on my lap.

"Sure," Chloe smiles. She's clad in a frilly top with hip-hugging jeans and brown suede boots. Her wavy, caramel hair is pulled loosely back at the nape of her neck. Bangs wisp her eyes.

I've never had dinner with such gorgeous and successful people before. Andrew's mom looks like Barbie and works as a college professor. Andrew's dad is Ken and is some politician in town. Even Andrew's grandfather is good looking with Andrew's chiseled face and matching dimples. Oh yeah, he's a retired judge.

Andrew and I shared the most amazing November so far. After Fall Brawl, we settled into this girlfriend-boyfriend routine. Soccer and football practice, then hang out and finish our homework together at my house. When I had a soccer game, he'd catch the end after his football practice. Afterwards, he'd walk me home. Every Saturday, I watched his football games with Lizzy; afterwards, we'd watch movies at his house. That's why I'm skipping basketball this season. To continue feeling normal. Continue being Andrew's girlfriend with no silly sports interruptions.

For the past week, I've dodged the basketball coach like a soccer striker faking out a defender. He's not thrilled about my decision and I've yet to break the news to mom and dad. It's not like basketball is my favorite sport anyway.

I catch a whiff of Andrew's freshly showered scent. His arm hairs tickle my forearm as he bends over, fork-shoveling turkey and potatoes into his mouth. Even stuffing his face, he's still hot.

He snags me staring at him, smiles, and grabs my knee with his utensil free hand. I shiver.

"What is your favorite subject, Ashley?" Andrew's mom asks smiling gently.

"I really like gym." Not a good answer, try again. "Oh and writing class. I really like writing class."

"I used to love writing class, too. I teach writing at the college."

I smile. Jackpot.

"So, Andrew, ready for the season?" Andrew's uncle asks. "Midnight practice, tonight, right?"

"Yup," Andrew answers and pulls his hand from my knee. "Can't wait to get out on the court."

"Isn't it hard to have to play a football game this morning and then practice basketball tonight?" Andrew's aunt chimes in.

"Nah. Basketball practice isn't mandatory for football players, but I like to be there. I love Thanksgiving. Football, then right to basketball. It's great," he says as he digs into his food again.

Andrew is the eternal optimist. Ask him if he's sad that the world is about to explode and he'll say, "But it will make spectacular fireworks."

After the yummy meal settles in our stomachs, Andrew and I help clear the dishes. The tryptophan begins to take effect, so Andrew takes my hand and leads me to the back den. Tons of windows enclose the den, which overlooks the bay. A big screen T.V. is mounted in the far corner of the room and on the opposite side of the window, a huge wrap-around couch covers the back wall.

We settle into our spot, a cozy corner of the couch, while Andrew channel surfs searching for the football game. He lounges back placing his arm around my shoulders. I snuggle into the nook.

"I can't believe I'll be driving in six months," Andrew says. He's car obsessed.

"Yeah, I know." For a brief moment, I picture Andrew and me cruising around Sunray Beach in a brand new Mercedes.

"So, what did you want to tell me?" Andrew asks.

"It's about basketball." I'm bursting.

"What about basketball?" he asks still staring at the game.

"I'm not playing this year." I say.

"What?" Andrew sits up. He unwraps his arm from my shoulders. "I thought you liked basketball. Plus, you're good."

"I do, but you even said, you love having me at all your games. It's been an amazing month. I don't want it to end. Once Spring rolls around, it will be nonstop softball again and I don't even want to think about what the summer will be like," I add.

"But, Ashley, we don't have to spend every second together. I mean, don't get me wrong, I like seeing you at my games, but I don't want you to change your life for me."

I hang my head and nibble on my nail. I thought he would love the idea. I was certain when I told him he would be ecstatic.

"I don't want to miss anything, like I did during the fall," I say.

"I know Ash. If you're sure about this, I guess it's okay. But, don't do it for me."

"The girls and boys games are exactly the same times and when you're at Sunray, I'm away. Softball winter practices start in January and are held on Sundays. We can hang out all week. It's perfect."

Just then, Chloe smacks Andrew on the back of the head and falls into the couch next to us. She grabs the remote.

Andrew scoots to the other side of the couch. I know it will be perfect. I'll be like Eva Longoria watching Tony Parker from the sidelines all season.

After Andrew's mom drops me off, I flop into bed and grab my cell.

"Hey, Ash, whaz up?" Lizzy says.

"I told Andrew I'm not playing basketball and he wasn't exactly thrilled."

"What? I thought he would be super psyched to hear you'd be around more." I hear something in the background.

"I know. What are you watching?"

"Nothing, I'm online, working on my MySpace."

"I really need to work on mine. Maybe add some pictures of Andrew and me."

Now that I'll be home more, I'll have plenty of time to do normal stuff.

"What did he say?" Lizzy asks.

"That's my point. He really didn't say anything. He was all over me, then I told him about basketball and he didn't touch me the rest of the night." Thinking about the night causes a serious case of nail biting.

"Maybe he had turkey gas and didn't want to sit too close to you."

"Very funny, Liz," I say.

"Mark's been acting pretty strange too."

I would never tell Lizzy this, but Mark always acts strange. "Did he go to practice tonight?"

"Yeah, he left my house around nine. Said he wanted to rest before practice."

"Guys are weird." I get up to turn on the computer.

"Are you online?" Lizzy asks.

"I'm getting on now," I say. "I haven't been online in ages." Too busy juggling sports and my boyfriend. Three months off is going to feel amazing.

"Check out my page. I've been working on it since Mark left."

"Alright, I will."

I log on to my MySpace page. It's exactly the way I left it in August. I've been on, but I haven't had a chance to update it since before the summer. It's wall-to-wall softball with only one tiny picture of Andrew. The one I downloaded from my cell phone, the first night we hooked up. My life has certainly has changed since then. I add change MySpace page to my mental list of things to do now that I'm not playing basketball.

A couple of messages from friends, but nothing new or exciting. I switch to Lizzy's page.

"Looks good," I say. "I'll leave you a comment."

"Okay, Leave me something good and scandalous. Talk to you tomorrow, free woman. Want to go shopping?"

"Sure, call me when you wake up." I go back to MySpace.

Two hours of MySpace surfing later and my stomach is in my throat. Splashed over Megan's MySpace page are tons of pictures of her and my Andrew at the dance. No dancing pics, just her and Andrew posing with groups of people. Andrew's arm around her shoulders and Megan's nasty hands around his hips.

I decide to continue the torture. I type, Christina Mayer, Cape Town, in the search engine. Sure enough, Christy's Orange Crush page and pictures fill the screen. I click into her blog to see what's she's saying. I scroll down. Mentions of softball, games, Fall Brawl, and what? I read it again.

'I can't stand girls who think life is all about them. This fall, we acquired this new girl on our team. She's this princess. Always thinking everything is about her. Her hot boyfriend came to our game last weekend. He was totally checking me out the whole day. She's so oblivious because she too tied up in herself to notice.'

Is Christy talking about me? Was Andrew really checking her

out? He couldn't have been. I would have noticed. But, I was paying a lot of attention to Chloe that day. Totally star struck. I hate Christy.

Like a car accident you drive by and can't help staring at, I continue to surf through Christy's MySpace page. She has pictures of her and her grandmom. I never noticed before, but I've never seen her parents at a game. Does she live with her grandmother? What happened to her parents?

Her friends are everyone from fellow Cape Catholic students to thirty-something Shop n' Eat employees. I never knew she worked at the grocery store. I wonder if she works to pay for ASA?

My eyes are heavy. It's almost three a.m.; I log out of MySpace and shut down my laptop. I flip open my phone and text Andrew.

Fr: Ashley

Hope u had fun at practice. See u tomorrow happy turkey day :)

11/23/07   3:02 a.m.

I place my cell on my nightstand, fall into bed and hug my comforter. A tiny part of me misses the feeling of knowing I would be off to b-ball tomorrow. But, instead, I'll be shopping. Then, I can hang out with Andrew. That's why I'm doing this. Right?

"Hello?" I hold the phone and wipe the sleep out of my eyes.

The clock reads twelve ten. Lizzy is sobbing on the other

end of the line.

"He, he broke up with with..." she blubbers.

"What?" I sit up in bed.

"Mmmmark. He broke up with... with..."

I can't understand Lizzy through the sobs.

"He broke up with you?" I ask.

"Yes."

I'll be right over. I kick off the comforter and grab a towel off the floor.

Thirty minutes later I'm in Lizzy's bedroom hugging her.

"Why'd he do it?" I ask.

"He said he needed space. He wants more time to hang out. He said I'm smothering him. Whatever. I think he's got some skank on the side."

Lizzy begins to pull herself together. I'm a little concerned. I've really never witnessed a crying bout like earlier, but in the time it took me to get a shower and hightail it over here, she's back. No more tears.

"Are you okay?" I ask.

"I'm okay now. Let's get dressed and go over to the mall. I need to buy some new clothes and stuff. Screw Mark," she says.

I swear Lizzy is bipolar.

"I wasn't that into Mark anyway," she says.

I roll my eyes.

" Let's plan something good tonight. Is there a party some-where? Don't you know people from Cape Catholic? Why don't you call them and see what they're doing tonight?" she asks.

"Uh, Liz, I have plans with Andrew." I say.

"I'm your best friend and I need you," she says.

Lizzy would never ditch me for a guy, but I want to hang out with Andrew so bad.

After four hours of post-breakup shopping, I'm beat. I call Andrew for the fourth time since noon. Still voicemail. I leave my fourth message and text him for the third time. Why isn't he get-ting back to me? I slump against Lizzy's bed. Lizzy flings her shop-ping bags on her bed.

"Since you have your phone out," Lizzy says. "Why don't you call one of your softball girls?"

"Lizzy, it's probably..."

Lizzy sticks her outstretched hand in front of my face. "Live a little, Ashley. Let's do something new for a change."

I dial Maggie.

"Hey, Ashley. How are you?" she says.

"Hey, Mag. What's up," I answer.

"Nothing much. Do we have practice or something?"

"No, actually, I was calling to see if you wanted to hang out tonight with me and one of my friends." I look over at Lizzy who is staring at me.

"There's a party at Christy's tonight? Want to go?"

My stomach drops. "Uh, I don't know."

"I'm sure she would be cool with it if you showed up. I mean, we're a team. I think Kate is going."

Uh, no she hates me, she would not be cool with it. "I'm not really sure," I say as Lizzy's baby blues shoot darts at my forehead.

"Oh, don't be ridiculous. I'll pick you guys up at eight," she says. "Just give me directions."

I look over at Lizzy who is butt-hopping on the side of her bed grinning ear to ear. I give Maggie directions.

What have I gotten myself into? I'm supposed to be enjoying my weekend with Andrew. Instead, I'm going to a party at Christy's, who happens to hate my guts, with Lizzy, who is on a major rebound. This is going to be a major disaster.

Later that night, while I wait for Maggie, I check my phone. Lizzy is applying her fourteenth layer of black mascara. Still no Andrew. I called a fifth time, but decided to stop because it was getting ridiculous. He, obviously, like me, is hanging out with the other half of the bitter break-up, Mark. But still, not since September, have I gone a whole day without talking to Andrew.

I hear Maggie's car pull up. Lizzy does one last check in the mirror while adjusting her barely there skirt and tank. I'm clad in my usual jeans and a tee. I grab my jacket. Lizzy grabs nothing.

My mom reminds me of my ridiculously early curfew on the way out the door. We squish into the backseat of Maggie's mom's Sebring.

"Hi, Ashley," Stephanie says to me in the backseat. The first word Stephanie ever said to me. "This must be Lizzy," she mutters.

How does she know Lizzy? I guess it's a small island.

"Hi, Ash and Liz," Kate turns around to smile at us from the front seat squished between Maggie and her mom.

"Hey, Kate." I say.

"Hi," Lizzy says. She barely pays attention to Stephanie or Kate. Lizzy's too busy scheming her moves for the night.

It takes about five minutes to arrive at Christy's tiny bungalow on the west side of Cape Town. It's not as nice as some of the homes that sit on the bay or ocean, but it's decent. I'm assuming it's Christy's grandparents place after reading her MySpace page.

I'm still not sure how Christy is going to handle seeing me as I make my way to the front door. Pumping beats echo from the petite place. A stumbling boy makes his way out of the front door almost running over Maggie. She scrunches her nose and ducks out of his way, just in time. He stumbles past and pukes in a bush.

We break out in giggles. Lizzy grabs my arm, "Before we go in, how do I look?" she asks.

For the millionth time I say, "You look good, Lizzy."

"Uh oh," I hear Kate say. She turns toward Lizzy attempting to stop her from going in.

Lizzy steps into the living room in front of me and stops. I peek around her and spot Mark with his arm around Christy. Christy is beaming from ear to ear with her hand cupping Mark's butt. They're both talking to Andrew and a couple of girls.

Mark must have heard Kate because his eyes meet Lizzy's. If looks could kill, Mark would have met the most horrible death known to mankind at that moment. He pulls his arm back from around Christy's shoulder. Christy looks up at Mark then follows his gaze toward us.

I grab Lizzy's hand because I know what her first reaction is and as much as I would love to see her kill Christy, I know it just won't be good. Andrew becomes aware of the situation and turns to face us. His face drops when he sees me.

"Who is that slut you have your scummy hands on," she screams. Lizzy looks at me.

"Is that the same Christy that is always giving you a hard time?" She turns back to Christy and Mark. She lunges at them.

By this time, the entire party, including Andrew, is staring at us. No talking, just stares with some vintage Green Day song playing in the background.

I grab Lizzy before she kills the couple and pull her out the door.

"Let's kick her ass for good," she screams as she stomps out into the yard. Tears fill the corners of Lizzy's eyes.

"Lizzy, come on, they're not worth it. Let's get out of here," I say.

"Lizzy, wait," The door slams as Mark jogs down the steps. Andrew is behind him. Lizzy turns and sprints down the street with Mark scurrying after her. Andrew stands at the door, stares at me for a second, and retreats back into the party with his head down.

I watch as Mark catches up to Lizzy. He grabs her by her bicep as Lizzy cold cocks Mark in the jaw. He shakes it off and follows her. I know the drill, so I find a seat on the curb and wait. No way am I going back into that house after Lizzy's explosion. But, I would love to know why the hell Andrew didn't talk to me.

I pull out my cell phone and call Andrew. No answer. Doesn't he have his cell phone with him? What the f? Why isn't he talking to me or answering my calls?

I go over my choices. I could, (a) go back into the house and grab Andrew to talk, hoping Christy and her cronies will even let me in or (b) walk home and talk to Andrew later.

I begin to haul my butt home. It's only eight o'clock. What a night.

After a few blocks, I pull out my cell again.

"Hey," a voice whispers from behind me.

I jump, toss my phone, and turn around to face Jake.

"Why is a pretty girl like you walking alone on a Friday

night?" Jake asks.

I smile, phew; it's not a rapist. "Nothing. Just waiting for Lizzy," I answer while I pick up my phone.

"Lizzy drama tonight, huh?" Jake says. "Where's pretty boy?"

"I don't know," I answer. "What are you doing?" Trash bags peak out of a Sunray Beach wrestling sweatshirt and sweatpants.

"Cutting weight for wrestling. I'm trying to get down to one-twenty-five," he answers.

"With trash bags?" I ask.

"You sweat more," he says. "If you were my girlfriend, I would be hanging out with you all the time, not watching you leave a party and walk Cape Town all by yourself in the dark."

I smile back at him.

"See you on Monday." He dashes down the street.

"Good luck," I say.

I spend the rest of the weekend freaking out. I call Andrew's cell a couple more times. Nothing. Three straight days and no Andrew. He's not the type of guy to not call me back.

Tough talking Lizzy spent the whole night working things out with Mark. She says they're friends. Yeah right, more like friends with benefits. I never pegged Lizzy as the type to take someone back who obviously is into someone else. She says she loves him and he promised he was done with Christy. Whatever.

"I didn't know you were still there. I thought you left with Lizzy and Mark," Andrew says before homeroom on Monday.

"Come on, Andrew. You saw me," I say.

"Ashley, I told you, I had to hang out with Mark. He was really confused over the whole Lizzy thing."

"So, you couldn't call me back? And anyway, he was with Lizzy." I say.

"I was busy with basketball and school work," he answers.

"On a holiday weekend? That's such bullshit," I say.

"Why don't you believe me?"

Because you're acting like a jerk.

"I just don't. It's strange. You always call me back. Plus, we always hang out," I say.

Andrew swings his arm around my shoulders. I slink underneath his hold.

"Come on, Ashley. We had such a nice Thanksgiving. It's no big deal if I don't call you for a couple of days. I was just busy. I think you're just freaked out about Lizzy and Mark. You know, we're not them. It's like you're acting like I was the one hooking up with someone behind your back."

Am I overreacting? Maybe I am just freaking out because Mark was messing around on Lizzy.

His face is close to mine as he nibbles my ear then kisses my lips. Shivers run up and down my spine.

Bottom of the Fourth
December, Freshman Year

Paul McCartney's voice fills my pine tree scented house. My mom's belting out "Simply Having a Wonderful Christmas Time" from her bedroom.

"What are you doing, Ashleeeeey?" Max, the human hyena, screams and pounds on my locked bedroom door. "Are you wrapping my gift?" he asks for the millionth time since November.

"Max, I'll be out in a minute," I yell. It's almost five-o-clock. Normally, I would still be at basketball practice, but instead I'm stuck in this house.

I put the finishing touches on Andrew's presents and shove them under my bed. I searched the mall for two straight days and decided on a Notre Dame jersey and new football. It's pretty easy to spend so much time shopping when your boyfriend is M.I.A.

Yup, ever since Christy's party, I swear Andrew avoids me

like a pitcher avoids throwing a meatball to the best batter on the opposing team. I mean, we still see each other at school, but weekends he's always "busy". Busy with Mark, busy with basketball, busy hanging out with the guys, busy my ass.

"Jingle Bells" vibrates on my night stand.

"Hello?"

"Hey, Ash, it's Liz."

"What's up?" I ask.

"Do you want to hang out tonight?"

"Sure. Why don't we go to the basketball game? I want to surprise Andrew."

See, this is my plan. I'm going to surprise Andrew and see what his problem is. Kind of a last ditch effort to see what's going on.

"Let's do something different tonight."

I really want Lizzy to be there.

"Yeah, Liz, but it's Mainland."

"So? Come on, Ashley, let's catch a movie or something," she says. "I'm sick of sitting at basketball games."

I never get tired of watching sports. Playing, watching, reading about... I love sports.

"Really, Liz. I want to try to go to the game and talk to Andrew. Can't we catch a movie after the game or another night?" I plead.

"You are really losing it, Ash," she says.

"What are you talking about," I ask.

"Come on, Ash. Andrew is blowing you off. When is the last time Andrew took you out or you two spent time together separate from a basketball court or school?" she asks.

I think back. But, he's busy with basketball. Lizzy just doesn't get it; she's not a real athlete. Athletes have to make sacrifices. But, she does have a point. That's why I'm determined to go tonight. To find out what the hell's going on.

"Lizzy, it's complicated," I answer after a pause.

"Whatever, Ash. Just watch yourself. Don't turn into one of those pathetic chicks that sit around waiting for a guy. That so isn't you," she says.

"I'm not one of those girls. I still go to softball on Sundays."

"Think about tonight," she says and hangs up.

I call Andrew.

His voicemail picks up. It's almost five; he must be on the bus.

"Ashley, dinner time," my mom calls from the kitchen.

I stroll down the hallway and sit down next to my dad. "Hey dad, can you take me to Andrew's game tonight?" I ask.

My mom lets out a deep breath.

"Why don't you workout tonight with me instead?" he pleads. "I'm going to the station gym, tonight, Ash. It'll be fun."

"Can't you drop me off on your way? I can catch a ride

home with Mr. and Mrs. Sinclair," I say.

"You really need to prepare for the season, Ash," he adds.

I roll my eyes and stab my steak with my fork. Why isn't anyone cooperating?

"Why don't you help me decorate tonight, Boo," my mom asks. "Christmas is only one week away."

"Tempting, mom, but no. I'll call the Sinclair's to see if I can hitch a ride with them," I say.

The rest of the dinner consists of Max stammering on and on about Christmas and what he wants from Santa Claus.

After dinner, I return to my room. It's absolutely spotless. All I do is clean, visit MySpace, and go to Andrew's games. My glove stares at me from my chair, so I toss it into the closet.

I call Andrew's house. Chloe answers.

"Hey Chloe, did your parents leave for Andrew's game, yet?" I ask.

"They already left," she says. "What's up, Ashley? Haven't seen you in a while."

"I'm good. Are you going to the game tonight?" I ask.

"No, not tonight. I'm going to hit the mall," she says.

"Have fun."

"I will," she says.

Great, now I'm stuck at home. Should I go workout with my dad to make him happy, decorate with my mom to make her happy, or hang out with Lizzy. I log onto my computer.

"You are not taking a bus to Andrew's game." My dad blocks the front door holding his POLICE duffel bag.

"Well, no one will take me and I can't drive," I say.

"Argh. Ashley, you can miss one stinking game." His face is red.

"No, I can't. This is how Andrew and I connect."

"You're not going to win," my mom says from the kitchen.

"Get in the car, Ashley," my dad relents.

I skip toward the convertible.

When I arrive at the game, the second period is just starting. I scan the crowd for the Sinclair's. I locate them sitting on the top bleacher by their designer duds .

I hop the bleachers two at a time and park myself next to Mrs. Sinclair.

"Hi, Ashley, how are you," she beams. Her warmth radiates.

"Hi, Mrs. Sinclair, I'm fine. How are you?" I ask.

"Just wonderful. We're up by eight. Andrew scored four in the first," she answers.

"Awesome. Hi, Mr. Sinclair," I say.

Mr. Sinclair grins showing his Sinclair family dimples, "Hi, Ashley, great to see you," he says.

I settle next to Mrs. Sinclair and scan the court for Andrew. There he is. Looking hot as usual.

"So, Ashley, are you getting ready for the holidays?" Mrs. Sinclair asks.

"Yeah, I can't wait. I just bought Andrew's gift yesterday."

She grins. "What are you getting your mom and dad?" she asks.

"The usual. I'm getting mom a gift certificate to a book store and a sweater and dad's getting a gift certificate to a car store," I answer.

"That's sweet of you," she says. The crowd erupts. I look down at the court to see Andrew jogging back to defend. Seeing him makes it all worth it.

The final buzzer screams and both teams line-up to slap hands. Sunray blew out Mainland, 54-30. A pretty boring game. I stand up to stretch.

"Do you need a ride home?" Mrs. Sinclair asks.

"Yes, please, do you mind?"

"Not at all, sweetheart," she says and grins.

I hop the bleachers to catch a moment with Andrew. He's bent over a chair, towel in hand, wiping the sweat off his face.

"Hi," I say. "Great game."

"Thanks," he mutters. He places the towel in his bag, swings the bag over his shoulder, and turns toward the locker room.

I grab his arm. "Andrew," I say.

"What?" he turns around to face me.

"I came here to see you play. Can't you say more than, "Thanks?" I say.

"Look, Ash. Wait for me after the game, I want to talk to you," he says and turns around. He trots into the locker room.

Finally, he wants to talk and straighten things out. At least now I can find out what his problem is. I breathe a sigh of relief and catch up with the Sinclairs.

After thirty minutes of Christmas conversation in the back-seat of the Sinclair's white Mercedes, I'm bursting with excitement. No Mark, no basketball. Just him and me. Maybe, he'll be back to the old Andrew.

The tires beat a rhythm as they roll over the bay bridge. I stare at the white salt ice caps forming over the shallow water. As we near the school, white and multicolored lights light the dark sky as big blow-up Santa Clauses and Grinches spawn lawns.

We roll into Sunray's parking lot just as the bus arrives behind us. The basketball team unloads. As always, Andrew is the second to the last one off the bus.

Andrew's head is down as he treks toward the car. He's back in his pre-basketball clothes, a light brown sweater and khaki's.

I want to bust out of the car and give him a giant hug. I'm starving to feel his arms around me. It's been too long.

He grabs for the passenger door. Opens it. I sit up straight and give him my best smile.

He looks at his parents. Then, he swings his bag on the car floor. "I'm going to walk Ashley home. Then, I'll call Mark for a ride. Okay?" he says.

Andrew's parents give each other a funny look. "Sure, Andrew. Great game. See you at home," his dad finally says.

I scoot across the leather seat. I can't wait to be alone with him and talk, make things normal again. I hop to my feet.

"Hey. It's been a while since we've been alone," I babble.

"Yeah," he says.

His parents take off. Mark drives by and yells something that sounds like, good luck, out the window. Good luck for what? Tomorrow's game?

Andrew begins to walk in front of me.

"Are you coming?" he asks.

Of course, I am.

I practically run next to him, sliding my arm around his waist.

"Great game, Andrew," I say. Hoping to transform his yucky mood.

"Thanks. How's pitching? Doing much lately?" he asks.

Why is he asking me about pitching? Of course, I'm still pitching.

"On Sundays. But, I haven't really gone in the last couple of weeks," I say.

"Why?" he asks.

What are you, my mom?

"I don't know. Been busy with Christmas. Plus, I've got other things to do." I smile.

"Oh," he replies.

I wrap my arm tighter around his waist. My thick grey wool sweater isn't stopping the bitter beach winds.

Andrew digs his hands into his pockets. Why isn't he wrapping his arms around me?

"It's cold," I say.

"Yup," he says as he glances up toward the sky.

Suddenly, he stops moving.

"Ashley, we need to talk."

"About what?"

"Us."

"What about us?"

"It's just not working."

"What?" I say. "What do you mean it's not working? It's not working because you hang out with the guys too much. That's what's not working."

My stomach flips. I feel like I'm going to puke. I didn't do anything.

"We're not working anymore, Ashley. This isn't working," he stares at his shuffling shoes.

"But, I thought we were going to spend all sorts of time together. You told me in the fall, you couldn't wait for the winter because I'd be done with softball for a while and everything."

He's silent.

"This isn't fair, Andrew. I didn't do anything," I plead.

"I know, Ash. It's just one of those things," he says.

What the hell does he mean by that?

I can't stop the explosion as my emotions erupt.

"Is this about Megan? Do you want her? I knew it. Even Jake told me I was stupid to let you go to the dance with her."

"No, Ashley. This has nothing to do with Megan. It's me. It's you. We had fun. Now, it's over."

I feel like I can't breathe. Like I'm up to bat and took a pitch to the chest. This can't be happening.

"I'm sorry." He continues to stare at his shoes.

I don't want to cry in front of him so I swallow a massive lump in my throat. This isn't fair. My body fills with adrenaline. Hot tears fill the corners of my eyes. My lips begin to tremble. I want to scream, "No," but I stop. Instead, I turn around and run. I run until I can't run anymore. The cold air burns my throat. I run for blocks and blocks until I reach the beach, the dunes. Our dunes. I sit next to a dune and the tears spill, spill onto the sand.

I lose track of time until my cell phone vibrates. I flip it open to look. It's Andrew. I close it. What can I possibly have to say to him? My head throbs. My tears are dried up. No more left to lose.

I stand up and trek toward home. Lizzy was right. My parents were right. I was losing myself. I vow I will never, ever, give anything up for a guy again. Ever.

When I arrive home, I march straight to my room. Andrew's freshly wrapped present stares at me from underneath the bed, and his hoody hangs over my chair. I swallow a lump in my throat.as I remove the reminders of Andrew from my room.

First, the present. I shove it into the back of my closet. The newly wrapped paper shreds as I push it farther and farther back until I can't see it anymore.

Next, I grab Andrew's hoody and toss it on top of the present. I grab old clothes and pile them on top of the memories. I spot my glove on the closet floor. I pick it up and place it on my desk. I promise to return to pitching as soon as possible. Softball doesn't hurt like this. I collect every picture of Andrew and shove each one in the back of the closet. I'm done.

I rearrange my room. Picture frames of Andrew are replaced with trophies and balls. My autograph and framed picture with my softball idol, Jennie Masterson is placed back on my nightstand.

When I'm finished, I pick up a softball, sit on my bed, and spin it. I practice wrist snaps under my leg while I cry. When I'm finally exhausted, I sleep.

Top of the Fifth
January, Freshman Year

It's the day before my fifteenth birthday. A birthday I was supposed to spend with Andrew. It's a miracle I've managed to avoid Andrew in this small school for a straight month by taking alternate routes to classes, moving my lunch spot, and talking to my last period teacher after school to stall until the hallways clear. Andrew never called again after that night. I kind of wish he had, but it's probably best. I think if I heard his voice, I'm afraid I'd freak and want him back.

If I had basketball to take my mind off him, I'd probably be over this knot in my stomach, but instead I'm throwing all my heartache into softball. Pitching four times a week plus ASA practice. I'm determined to become the best Sunray softball player ever.

Christmas sucked. I holed myself in my room for the entire Christmas break. I spent most of the time choking back tears and slinging my softball while putting on a happy face for all the relatives that love to visit the beach when it's minus twenty degrees.

Lizzy managed to pull me out of my pity party once to go shopping, but I was totally miserable and moped through every store. Eventually, she gave up and didn't bother me again until January.

Lizzy and Mark are still friends with bennies. Both hook up with other people, but if they want to hook up with each other, then they do. I think Mark's getting his cake and eating it to. But, Lizzy says it was her idea. Yeah, right.

Lizzy did find out after grabbing Mark's phone and reading his texts during study hall, that he was seeing Christy on the side this fall. Which probably explains some of Christy's hatred toward me. Guilt by association with Lizzy.

"Hey, Ashley," Jake greets me with a grin every day in homeroom. He is a good distraction. A complete opposite of Andrew except for his dimples.

"Hi," I say.

"How's my favorite freshman?" he asks like he does everyday. Jake twitches in his seat while clutching a paper cup. He spits in it all day while sucking on candy. Says it helps him make weight for wrestling. Jake's cup is filled with reddish slobber. Today's candy of the day must be of the red variety.

"Fine," I say. I can't help myself, and I grin at Jake. Rumor has it he's messed around with half the freshman girls and a couple of upperclassman. I never asked him, but I am curious. I mean, he's only fourteen.

"Are you over pretty boy, yet?"

Did I mention that everyone knows about the break-up with Andrew? Our town is so tiny. The buzz is Andrew hooked up with Megan at Christy's party. That's why he was MIA and eventually broke up with me because of a guilty conscience. Truth or tabloid, I still want to kill both Megan and Andrew. Plus, I feel like a complete dumb ass for staying with him even after he went to the dance with Megan. But, thinking of him still makes my stomach do somersaults. Go figure.

"Yeah, I guess," I say.

"Remember, you always have me," he smiles.

Homeroom drags, school drags, days drag. It's torture being cooped up at the same school with Andrew and having to avoid him. Like a detective, I spend hours trying to decipher the words he said to me on the night of the break-up bombshell and try to figure out what went wrong.

The bell rings. I grab my books. Jake sneaks up next to me.

"You know, my match is tonight at seven," he says. Jake is a varsity wrestler. I heard he's an animal on the mat, but I've never seen a high school wrestling match. I don't get that sport, all the twisting, torture, and dog-on-dog humping.

"Yeah, so what?" I remind him that I'm not some middle school chick lining up to suck face and do whatever with him because he wins a few wrestling matches.

"Why don't you come to my match?" he asks with matching Andrew big brown eyes.

"I might check it out. If I'm not busy," I say.

He smirks and spits in his cup.

As I contemplate going to the match on my way to my locker, I'm not paying attention to my Andrew avoidance plan, and I end up face to face with him. Megan is smack next to him. Andrew and I jockey side to side, trying to get by each other, but instead we wind up face to face again. He looks like a batter who gets caught in a run down.

"Sorry," he mutters as he passes me by.

Sure, you're sorry. Sorry, for ruining my Christmas and basketball season. When I see Andrew it's bad enough, but seeing him with Megan is like ripping my heart out in the middle of the hallway and stomping on it until it stops beating for the world to see. Happy birthday to me.

"Stay away from Jake. He's a total dirtball," Lizzy says as we're walking home from another heart-wrenching day at Sunray. Walking home passes the time. Passes the time until softball season.

"How do you know he's a dirtball?" I ask.

"Oh come on, Ashley. He just is. He broke Kaitlin's heart. Remember her crying about it on the bus on our way to soccer?"

I faintly recall Kaitlin complaining about Jake, but she fessed up on the bus during soccer that she did some heavy stuff with him like after two weeks of dating. She shouldn't have offered her services so quick. And when she did, she followed him around like a puppy dog. He was done, lost interest. She should have known better.

"I just want to watch some wrestling. It's no big deal," I say.

Lizzy looks at me out of the corners of her eyes. "I've heard that one before," she says.

"I'm in total control now. No boyfriends. I will not let myself fall for someone like I did Andrew. I have a scholarship to win and a season coming up," I say.

"Whatever," Lizzy says.

"Come on, check it out with me," I beg. "I heard there are tons of hot guys on the team. It'll get your mind off of Mark and his 'let's be friends,' bull."

When it comes to hot, new guys, Lizzy can't resist.

"I can't believe you talked me into this," Lizzy says as she nibbles on a piece of licorice.

The gym is packed. Loud music blares from the speakers as fifty or so guys clad in black sweatpants and hoodies jog around a huge yellow square mat. They stop in unison, jog in place, and begin their stretch routine. Lizzy and I shuffle to find a seat. The gym's packed.

"I had no idea wrestling is so huge," I scream so she can hear me over the music.

"I know. Look at that one," Lizzy points with her licorice to a ripped guy with dark hair and light eyes jumping rope on the visitor's side.

I have to admit, the guys do look hot. There's something about guys fighting each other. Plus, it takes guts to grapple with another guy in front of a huge crowd. Sure, it takes guts to pitch, but I have eight girls helping me out. Wrestlers are on their own. At the end of the stretch routine, the wrestlers pile in a human mountain in the middle of the mat. They chant, "Team," and bounce back to their feet.

The refs and coaches converse at the scorer's table. Both teams line up as individual matches are announced.

Lizzy's eyes are glued to the mat. Like me, she is enthralled by the spectacle.

"I didn't know there were so many hot guys at Sunray," she says.

Jake is up next. A loud cheer erupts when they announce Jake's undefeated record. He pulls his hood up over his head and shakes hands with a short and stocky mean-faced guy in the center of the mat. Jake keeps his hood up and jogs in place behind his teammates. He grabs a jump rope.

"Oh, great look who's here." Lizzy rolls her eyes and points to Mark standing by the side door. Behind Mark, I spot Andrew and Megan. What is he doing here? Why is Megan with them?

I keep my eyes glued to the mat. I don't want Andrew to know how uncomfortable he makes me feel.

They're coming this way. I take a deep breath, adjust my top, and sit up straight.

"Hi, Lizzy," Mark says first. Lizzy ignores him. I guess this week the friends thing isn't working.

"Hi," I quickly glance their way, then try to refocus on the wrestling match.

"Hi, Ashley," Megan purrs, taking Andrew's hand. The gym begins to spin.

Lizzy squeezes next to me. I shift over so Andrew, Mark, and Megan can squish behind Lizzy and I.

"Come, on, Andrew," I hear Megan say.

"Not right now." I can barely hear Andrew. He's speaking soft, almost like he doesn't want me to hear him.

"Pleeeeaaaasssse," Megan whines.

"Not right now, later, when we're alone," he says.

Alone? They're alone? It's so obvious now. He always wanted to be with Megan. I stand up. The gym feels like its one hundred degrees. I have to get out of here.

"Where are you going, Ash?" Lizzy asks.

"Bathroom." I give Lizzy the look. She follows me.

I walk to the bathroom like one of the old ladies in town who pump their arms up and down, speed walking across the beach.

"What the hell is wrong with you?" Lizzy asks me after we dodge into a health classroom.

"Why didn't you tell me? Why didn't you tell me he's with her?" I shout.

"What? Oh, Megan. Mark says Megan won't leave Andrew alone since you guys broke up. It's nothing. Anyway, you never even asked me about Andrew. I thought you were totally over him."

Yeah, I wish.

"Then, why can't he tell her to leave him alone?" I ask.

"You know how guys are. If it's there and it's easy, why not? Come on, Ash, he knew he wasn't getting anything from you, so he went for an easy fix. Megan's an easy lay."

"So, they hooked up?" I can't battle the tears any longer.

"According to Mark, it doesn't mean anything to Andrew. She passes time," Lizzy says. "Come on, Ash. I didn't want to tell you because she's nothing to him. He really liked you. Megan's just a physical thing."

Lizzy hugs me.

"I want to go home," I say.

"No way, Ashley. If you leave, Megan will think she has Andrew. Go back, so Megan feels uncomfortable. Go back, so Andrew can see you're over him."

She's right.

"Come on, Ash. You're so much hotter than Megan. You should see how Andrew still looks at you. He still likes you, but it didn't work out with you guys. Andrew's gonna hook up. You're gonna hook up. You might as well get used to it," Lizzy pleads.

She grabs a napkin from the snack stand outside the classroom and dabs my eyes. She pulls out her lip-gloss.

"Now, put this on and smile."

I swipe the lip-gloss over my lips and pull my shoulders back. I follow Lizzy back to the bleachers. Andrew stares right into my eyes as I make my way up the steps.

I maneuver past Mark and sit down. Jake is jumping rope.

"Now wrestling one hundred and twenty-five pounds, Jake Cole."

The crowd goes wild. I stand up and clap. Andrew doesn't.

Jake crouches down and shakes hands with his opponent. Within a matter of seconds, he has the other guy in some painful looking move. Jake's back is so cut. He looks up at the ref as if to say, "He's pinned and I'm hardly trying." The ref smacks the mat.

"Pin."

I shoot up to my feet and cheer for Jake. The ref raises Jake's hand. He smiles, jogs back to the team, and receives congratulations from his coaches and teammates.

"He is really good," I say to Lizzy loud enough so Andrew can hear. "I guess I should go now."

"Aren't you going to stay for the rest of the meet?" Lizzy asks.

"No, I've seen what I came to see," I say as I stand up and

maneuver past Mark once again. I swing my white bag over my shoulder.

"Bye," I wave to Lizzy and Mark. Hopping down the steps, I stare at Jake who is pulling his sweats over his singlet. He waves. I hope Andrew sees this.

I realize when I walk outside that I don't have a ride because I was supposed to walk home with Lizzy, and I totally just left her in the dust. My dad's on duty tonight, so I call him. Minutes later, the squad car pulls up.

When I'm home safe in my room, tears once again reappear. If he wanted to be with Megan, why didn't he just tell me instead of wasting my time?

Why her? Is it her humongous boobs?

I flip my mattress on its side and begin to wrist snap a softball under my leg. If I had hooters like Megan, I couldn't pitch like I do. I throw harder and harder. Screw Andrew.

The next day, when I open my locker, a card hits my Uggs. I open in it, secretly praying it's from Andrew. It's sweet. It's small, one of those ninety-nine cent cards. A little bear on the front holds a Happy Birthday to You sign. Inside, it says, I hope your day is as sweet as you are. It's signed, "Love, Jake."

Bottom of the Fifth
February, Freshman Year

Jake taps me on my shoulder during history class. Because of our last names, Clarke, Cole, it's almost guaranteed, if Jake's in my class, he's behind me.

My head is resting between my arms as I'm daydreaming about good pre-breakup times with Andrew, staring at a Vietnam War flick we're supposed to be learning something from.

"Want to celebrate with me on Sunday?" Jake whispers in my ear. It sends chills down my back.

"What are you talking about?" I half turn around, to catch a glimpse of him.

"Do you want to celebrate with me or not?" he asks again. Out of the corner of my eye, I sneak a peek of his devilish grin.

"My brother will pick you up," he says.

I knew Jake had a brother. He was in Chloe's class. Like Jake, he was an absolute animal on the mat. I think he placed fifth in the State Tournament his senior year. He was only the Sunray wrestler in the history of the school to ever place in States. It was a huge deal.

"I'll let you know, later," I smirk.

I lower my head back in between my arms. What does Jake have up his sleeve now? I do know I'm rebounding big time, like a basketball off the backboard. A basketball that I should be dribbling everyday, instead of sitting home thinking about Andrew, the a-hole.

The bell rings and I collect my books. I feel Jake's electricity behind me.

"Are you going to keep me waiting?" he asks.

His thick chest muscles push his Ultimate Fighting Championship long sleeve tee out just right. His huge neck stretches the collar. He must be really muscular under that t-shirt. Stop right there, before you get yourself in trouble again. I compose myself.

"What do you mean help you celebrate? Celebrate what?" I ask while shoveling books into my tote. I swing it over my shoulder.

"To celebrate my season. And to get me ready for States. My brother is taking me to the tattoo parlor," he says.

Tattoo parlor? Oh no, that's on the list. The list of things my parents forbid me to do: tattoos, sex, drugs, drinking, piercings.

They'll never let me go.

"Uh, no, that's okay. I have to pitch on Sundays," I say as I squeeze past Jake.

He touches my arm. My stomach fills with butterflies, but different from Andrew. I used to feel safe and serene, kind of bored with Andrew, like I'm lazily sitting on the beach. When Jake is with me, I'm excited, like I'm on a roller coaster.

"You're not getting away that easy," he says. I'll pick you up in front of Mario's Pizza at three on Sunday. I know your practices are at ten and your parents will probably never let their precious Ashley inside a tattoo parlor." He lets go of my arm and grins at me.

What can I say?

I spot Andrew walking with Megan. He's staring at me.

"I'll see you on Sunday." I say a bit louder, hoping Andrew will hear me.

I'm in front of Mario's Pizza at two forty-five waiting for Jake and his brother. Just think, six short months ago, Andrew and I met and shared our first kiss. Now, I'm waiting for the biggest bad boy at Sunray to pick me up.

After watching "LA Ink" last night, I'm so curious about the whole tattoo thing. I wasn't really sure what to wear to a tattoo parlor. See on the show, they wear a lot of black, like those girls who always talk to Jake. I thought about trying out the all black thing, but I looked stupid, so, I went with my usual, jeans and a tee with a thick wool sweater and Ugg boots.

An enormous red hunk of junk pulls up. I remember Jake telling me about this car. A car big enough and cheap enough to hold their surf boards.

"Hey," Jake gets out of the car and scoots into the back seat. He's once again wearing something wrestling. This time, a Sunray Beach wrestling windbreaker.

I'm stunned at how much of a gentleman Jake can be. Maybe, he's not as bad as Lizzy thinks?

"Hi," I say as I maneuver my way into the front seat. It's one of those old torn leather front seats with no console in the middle.

"Hi, Ashley, I'm John," he says.

"Hi, John," I squeak. John and Jake look like twins. While Andrew looks more like Zach Efron with brown eyes, Jake and John could pass as that hot guy with the buzz cut on the show, "Prison Break".

"So, Ashley, I've heard a lot about you," John says.

Really? Did he ever talk about the other girls? Or just me?

"Like what?" I decide to play the game.

"Well, for one thing, I heard you're hot, and I have to say, for once my brother is right," he says. He eyes me up and down, tilts his head, and grins.

He, too, has dimples. *Yum.*

"Thanks," I say. So, Jake thinks I'm hot? He's silent in the backseat.

It takes us less than ten minutes to arrive at the tattoo parlor. As we pull up, a squad car drives by. I sink into the seat, ducking underneath the dashboard. I hope Dad didn't see me.

"You okay," Jake asks.

"Fine. I slid on the leather," I lie.

Jake and John exchange glances.

The parlor is a black, painted, cement building in the touristy section of town. In big, red, thick letters the words Tattoo Gallery cover a huge sign hanging over the door.

We climb out of the car and walk toward the front door. Jake opens it for me. I walk inside. Millions of tattoo sketches shower the walls.

A multi-colored tattooed woman, greets us at the counter. Her hair is jet black, and her lip is pierced along with her cheeks, eyebrows, and ears. I scan her skin looking for a spot missing ink. Tattoos of portraits, names, dates, animals, rainbows, suns, and moons cover her body. Her skin looks like its been used as a doodle pad.

"Can I help you?" Her voice is hoarse.

"Yeah, my brother wants a tattoo," John answers. "It's to celebrate his wrestling season."

"Ohhh, cool. So, what are you thinking of getting?" she asks.

"Tribal. I want some sort of black tribal symbol around the top of my bicep," Jake answers as he runs his finger along the top of his arm. I wonder if it will hurt.

I'm so totally out of place here. But, the parlor is exciting, so many people getting so many different tattoos.

"Hmmm. How about this?" She points to tons of tribal tattoos covering the wall next to the window.

A buzzing sound hums from behind the counter. It sounds like a tooth drill. Ouch.

"Which one do you like, Ashley?" Jake asks.

He wants me to pick out his tattoo? I'm both flattered and terrified. I haven't even kissed this boy yet and he wants me to pick something that will be a permanent fixture on his body?

"Oh, I don't know Jake, get whatever you like?" I say.

"I want your opinion," he grins.

Jake, once again, casts this magical spell on me. I walk over to the tattoo drawings and choose the one I like best. How does he always gets me to do things I wouldn't normally do?

"Okay, I'll go with that one," Jake says.

"Come with me," she wiggles her finger toward us. "Sit here," she points to a wooden chair.

Another guy is getting what looks like a baby's face tattooed on his back. Freckles and hair cover his flab. A guy, also covered in ink, is holding what looks like a metal tooth drill with a tiny needle on the end. He dips the buzzing needle in black ink, runs it over the guy's skin, and then wipes blood and ink with a paper towel. He does this over and over again.

Jake sits down and the tattooed woman begins to work her magic. Jake doesn't flinch as she dips, buzzes, and wipes. It doesn't look so bad. My dad always told me his tattoo hurt like hell. Someday, I'd like to get a softball on my foot or ankle.

John reads my mind, "Want one?"

Jake interrupts. "She's a good girl, John. Leave her alone."

I smile. So, Jake thinks I'm a good girl. Something about the atmosphere I guess, but I'm dying to show them I'm not.

After an hour and a half of straight buzzing, Jake is done. I'm totally mesmerized by Jake. All that blood and ink and not once did he flinch. The woman hands him a mirror.

"So, what do you think?" she asks.

"Love it. Ashley, what do you think?" he asks.

"It looks good," I say. It does. It looks hot. Black thick tribal lines swim around his cut bicep.

The woman bandages Jake up, John pays, and we're back in the car. Jake's excitement is palpable.

"I can't wait to get back out on the mat tomorrow. This is what I needed to win the state championship," he says.

Jake and John begin a ten-minute talk about States. I stare out my window.

John stops in front of Mario's.

"Thanks, for bringing me. It was fun," I say.

"Anytime, Ashley," John says.

I hoist myself out of the heap. Jake climbs out of the back seat behind me.

"I'll walk you," he says.

"Oh, that's okay, it's only four blocks,"

"I know. But you can't walk alone. You're too pretty," he says. "Some guy might pick you up and want you for himself."

"Jake, it's the dead of winter. Nobody is here."

He waves to John and shuts the passenger door.

The salt air is pungent and frigid. I wrap my sweater around me. Jake takes off his wrestling windbreaker and hands it to me.

"Take this," he says.

"No, no, that's okay." No way, am I accepting clothes from a boy again.

"Take it," He begins to pull it over my head.

He's grinning ear to ear like the Joker. "Why are you so happy?" I ask him.

"I'm high," he answers.

High? When could he have possibly taken drugs? He's crazier than I thought. The rumors are true. "What are you on?" I ask.

"Not high on drugs. High on life. I would never, ever take drugs, Ashley." His face is suddenly serious.

I'm filled with relief. He walks backwards in front of me.

"What are you doing?" I ask.

"I want to study your beautiful face. So, instead of walking next to you, I'm walking in front of you so I can look at you."

My cheeks feel hot. Jake has made me feel scared, excited, and cheery in a mere minute. His eyes pierce mine. His energy radiates through my body. I think I want to kiss him, but I'm terrified. Normal Ashley, the sporty Ashley, interrupts my thoughts, and I push the kiss out of my mind.

He walks in front of me for blocks. It's kind of nice because he's blocking the frigid wind.

"So, how'd you get so good at wrestling," I ask.

"Let's just say, I've been fighting since I was a toddler."

"What do you mean?" I ask.

"Nothing. I guess the same way you got so good at sports. A lot of practice. So, what's next for you?"

"Well, I'll go home, probably eat dinner.."

"No, I mean, what's next for your life? Like, what's next after Cape Town?"

"Oh, I don't know, Jake. Right now, I just want to get through the softball season. I live life one sports season at a time."

"Well, I don't. I can't. I'm determined to get out of this hellhole and my ticket is wrestling. If I place in States, then colleges will start to notice. If I don't get a scholarship, no college for me."

Never in a million years would I have guessed goofy Jake was hiding plans to go to college. I mean he's not an honors student.

But come to think of it, he doesn't do bad in school. No wonder, he's always asking me about my homework.

"This is it," I say as we turn onto my street.

"I know where you live. See you tomorrow. It was fun sharing this tattoo with you. I'll remember you forever," he says.

He doesn't even wait for me to say anything. He's off sprinting down the street. What a screwball.

Top of the Sixth
February, Freshman Year

"You're not seriously thinking of going out with Jake to-night, are you?" Lizzy asks me in the hellish hallways on our way to math class.

"What's the big deal?" I ask.

"It's Valentines Day. That's the big deal."

"So?" I say.

"So. Valentines Day is a big deal. If you go out with Jake tonight, you might as well be dating him," she says.

Hmmm. What's so bad about dating Jake? I stay mum.

"Don't even go there, Ashley. He's a friggin' dirt ball."

"Well, I'm not with Andrew anymore. Anyway, Jake just passes time. What do you expect me to do, sit home?"

Why does Lizzy care so much about Jake? She doesn't even know him.

"Whatever, Ash," She plops down in her seat.

Three days ago, out of nowhere, Jake popped the V-Day question. It was a typical Monday for me, a total countdown until softball season. I wasn't even thinking about Valentines Day until I opened my locker and a rose was resting on top of my books. Underneath the rose was another one of those cheap cards from the dollar store. It read, "Will you make my Valentines Day special and hang out with me on Thursday? Love, Jake." He totally worked so hard on setting the whole thing up, how could I not say yes.

"Why don't you come with us? Jake's got a hot brother. Maybe he's available."

"No way, I wouldn't touch a Cole boy. Anyway, Mark and me are hanging out."

Are you kidding me?

"And you're bugging me about Jake? I thought you and Mark are just friends."

"We both didn't have anything to do for Valentines Day, so we're going to catch a movie or something."

Now it's my turn to sigh and plop in my seat.

Lizzy rolls her eyes. "At least, Mark hasn't messed around with half the class."

"Just Christy. And you need to give Jake a chance and stop judging him. You don't even know him."

By now, two girls between our seats are staring at us.

I don't care what anyone says. Jake is fun to hang out with.

And nothing is going to happen anyway. I'm so over guys.

The day drags. On my way to fifth period, I notice Andrew's locker is covered with pink and purple cut-out hearts and balloons. What the... ?

"Hi, Mrs. Miller. Can I have a pass to go to the bathroom?" I ask my writing teacher right after the bell rings.

"Sure, Ashley. Just put your homework on your desk," she smiles and hands me a pass.

I practically sprint out of class and return to the heart vomit all over Andrew's locker. A card hangs in the middle. I look around. The coast is clear. I open the card. "Love, Megan" in pink letters.

"What are you doing?"

Andrew is standing two feet away from me.

"Uh, nothing." I keep my eyes glued to the gray tile and practically jog to the bathroom.

I'm shaking as I duck into a stall. I'm so stupid. I remind myself that I'm over Andrew, right? Anyway, I'm going out with Jake tonight. But, I can't help but wonder, does Andrew talk and goof off with Megan the way he used to with me? Do they kiss on our spot on his couch in his family room? My heart sinks.

I stay in the bathroom until I think the coast is clear. Tiptoeing down the hallway, I sneak back into class.

"Is everything alright?" Mrs. Miller asks me as I take my seat.

"Yeah," I lie.

I check Megan out the rest of the day for signs of a Valentines Day present from Andrew. Nothing. I'll double check with Lizzy later to see if Andrew got her anything. That is, if she's still talking to me.

"Hey sweetheart." Jake's wearing a black UFC tee, sleeves rolled up, showing off his new tattoo, jeans, and his signature spit cup. His face is sunken in. Normally he weighs one hundred and fifty pounds; he cuts all the way down to one twenty-five. Miraculously, he's still hot, even though he looks manorexic.

"Are you ready for tonight?" he asks. "Make sure you dress warm and wear your sneakers."

He whips out a red rose from behind his back and hands it to me.

"Thanks, Jake."

"Another red rose for the prettiest girl on the East Coast." He hands it to me and walks toward his locker.

At the same time, Andrew turns the corner. His mouth drops. He walks in my direction, stopping in front of me. My stomach flops. He's going to say something about the locker incident earlier today. My cheeks are hot and probably as red as the rose I'm holding. Andrew parts his full lips.

"Jake's bad news," Andrew says.

"So's Megan," I snip.

"Just, be careful, Ashley," he says and walks away.

My heart pounds. My palms are sweaty. How dare he tell me how to live my life when he's totally banging the biggest slut at Sunray?

I'm supposed to meet Jake on the fourth street pier at seven. Dad was excited when I told him I was meeting someone to work out. He assumed it's a softball player. So, technically, I didn't lie. I didn't have to.

Walking down Fourth Street, I spot Jake spreading a red and white-checkered blanket across the wooden pier. A basket rests next to the blanket. He places a lit candle in the middle.

Jake is shuffling through the basket when I walk up. The sky is black with a white half-circle hovering over the crashing sea and white foam runs and retreats along the shoreline.

I'm shocked by Jake's obvious attempt at romance. Is this how he gets all these girls to do things with him? Well, not this chickie.

"Hey, Ashley. I'm so glad you're here." Jake stands up and smiles.

"Hi, Jake. This looks amazing," I say. I toss him his wrestling windbreaker.

"Thanks." Jake places a hand on the small of my back and guides me to the blanket. Every time he touches me, electricity shoots through my body, which I'm trying desperately to ignore.

"Sit, before it blows away."

I swore we were going to run. I never would have guessed he would plan a romantic dinner on the pier. I'm wearing my black and orange Crush warm-ups, ratty old running sneakers, a knit hat, gloves, and a scarf. Not exactly, a romantic dinner outfit.

Jake opens the basket and begins rummaging through it. He pulls out two bottles of water and tosses me one. Then, like a magician, he pulls out a sandwich for me and a salad for himself.

It's my favorite sandwich, turkey and cheese with a little bit of mayo, lettuce, and tomato, on a Kaiser roll. He totally pays attention, how cute.

"How did you know?" I ask.

"You eat turkey and cheese everyday for lunch," Jake answers.

He pulls out another rose identical to the one he gave me in school and hands it to me. "Happy Valentines Day," he says.

"Thanks Jake, this is so sweet."

"This is just the beginning." He says as he shoves a plastic forkful of lettuce into his mouth.

I take a bite out of the yummy sandwich and swig the water. Jake devours the salad and takes exactly two gulps of water.

"So, Ashley, tell me something about you that I don't already know," he says.

"What you see is what you get."

I'm not really feeling like opening up right now.

"Tell me more. What's one of your deep, dark Ashley secrets?

Like, did you ever miss a homework assignment?" Jake smiles and leans toward me.

"Whatever, Jake, I'm not that goody, goody. Anyway, my life is softball and sports," I say.

"You'll tell me more, soon." Without using his hands, Jake jumps up from a sitting position to his feet.

No way, slick man. I have sports to concentrate on. Next thing you know, I'll be making out with Jake and thinking about skipping softball again.

I finish my sandwich and take a few more swigs of water. Jake grabs my wrapper and his salad bowl and tosses them in the trashcan. After he folds up the blanket, he blows out the candle and places everything back into the basket. Jake picks up the basket and walks over toward a blue and white dirt bike. After he straps the basket to the back of the bike he hands me a helmet.

"Wanna ride?" he asks.

I've never been on the back of anything before, but I'm dying to find out what its like, so I grab the helmet and strap it on under my chin.

Jake climbs onto the dirt bike. I swing my leg over the bike and settle in behind him, wrapping my arms around his waist. He feels like he's wearing at least five sweatshirts. Must be cutting weight again. A jolt rushes through my body as he takes off.

I tuck my chin so my head doesn't swing backwards. We whiz down Ocean Drive. The beach stretches to our right. This is absolutely amazing.

Ocean Drive ends at the point, where the bay and ocean meet. He stops and switches the bike off. Jake climbs off. I follow.

"What are we doing?" I ask.

"Running. Ms. Athlete, Ashley. Now I have to work off that salad."

He takes off. Okay, I get the sneakers now. I take off.

He slows a bit so I can catch up. After five minutes, I'm breathing heavy.

Jake is in incredible shape. He jogs with no effort. I'm struggling. The cold wind cuts my throat and my legs begin to itch.

"How... much... longer..?" I gasp.

"I thought you are Ms. Athlete," he says. "We can turn around and jog back to the point."

"I can handle anything you dish out, Jake."

After another five minutes, which feels like five hours, I stop before I pass out.

He laughs. We turn around and walk back.

"Can I show you my spot?" Jake asks.

"Sure," I say not wanting the time with Jake to end. Not wanting to return home and think about Andrew.

I follow him through the dune grass to a sea grass free area by the water.

He sits on a pile of huge black rocks and pats a spot next to him.

I sit.

"I never thought a girl like you would accept an invitation from me, especially on Valentines Day," he says.

"Why not?" I ask.

"You're Ashley. The hot pitcher. I know what people say about me, Ash. The whole wrestler, dirt biker, tattoo guy. I mean, you usually date all-American pretty boys, like Andrew. I didn't think I had a chance."

"I guess you really don't know me." I say. We stare at each other. It's freezing. I scoot closer to him and shiver. A tingle runs through my body.

His eyes pierce mine. He begins to lean toward me and cups both cheeks with his hands.

Oh no, don't do it. Although there is nothing in the world I would like to do right now, I won't let myself fall for someone again and I feel myself totally falling for Jake. I could kiss him all night, but I turn my head to the side.

"Sorry, Jake," I say.

He stands up and begins walking toward his bike.

I get up and follow him. He picks up the pace.

When I reach him, he hands me the helmet and straddles his bike.

I begin to speak, but he revs the engine. I try to shout over it. I just want to explain. It's not him. It's me.

"Sorry, Jake. I just can't.."

"It's okay," he says.

We ride in silence all the way to my house. He drops me off around the corner, so my parents don't freak. He says nothing as he drives away. I hear the hum of the dirt bike engine grow softer.

I expected Jake to act differently toward me after that night. But, he didn't. It's weird. He totally acted like the same old Jake. But, he never asked me why I didn't kiss him. I even tried to explain once, but all he did was place his finger in front of my lips to stop me from talking. Then, he proceeded to blab on and on about his chances of making it to the State Championship.

Then, one day, I opened my locker and another cheap dollar store card fell out. This time, a cute bear covered the front and inside it said, "I'm not Andrew."

He's right, but I'm still Ashley.

After spending the last three months looking for stuff to do, I'm excited for the spring and another softball jam-packed schedule.

Dad, Kate, and I arrive at the indoor soccer field, which is converted to our winter softball practice space. It's forty-five minutes away and we make this trip three times a week during the winter months.

"Thanks, Mr. Clarke," Kate says as she climbs out of the convertible.

"Thanks, Dad," I add.

It's freezing inside the facility. Coach D is setting up pitching machines, tees, and nets across the field. A couple of girls are already working out with weights in the gym adjacent to the field.

"Hi, Ash. Hi, Kate," Coach D says.

"Do you need help?" Kate asks.

"Thanks, Kate. I'm okay. Grab a workout plan. We'll get started hitting in a few minutes."

Winter workouts are fun. We always hit the weights, then work on a specific skill, whether it's hitting, fielding, bunting, whatever. It's not like boring outside practices where we have to work on situations. I hate situational drills. Plus, during the off-season I can push myself without worrying about being weary for a game.

"Hey Mag," Kate says and joins Maggie at the leg press.

Christy is arm curling while Amy and Stephanie wait their turn by the machine. So, I walk over toward Maggie and Kate after grabbing the workout schedule.

"Ashley, I heard Andrew dumped your ass," I hear Christy cat.

"It was mutual," I lie.

Kate stares at me. She knows how devastated I was.

"That's not what I hear," Christy purrs. Amy giggles.

"How's Mark?" I shoot back knowing that Mark is snuggling

with Lizzy right now.

"You're friend is so stupid, thinking that boy is faithful. He's anything but," she cackles.

"Is she or are you stupid?" I say. Then, I regret it.

"I think you're the stupid one messing around with that dirtball, Jake," Christy says.

How the heck does she know what I do?

"Come on, guys," Kate interjects. "We're a team, knock this crap off."

"Yeah, what is the problem between you two anyway?" Maggie asks while getting in between Christy and I.

Before either one of us can answer, Coach D interrupts. "Okay, girls, let's get started. Maggie and Kate begin on the tees. Christy and Amy, follow me for the batting cages."

We glance at each other. It's going to be one long summer.

After a tension-filled, silent practice, Kate informs me she's going home with Maggie. I don't blame her. Kate's middle name is neutral.

"I don't think I want to play with the Crush this year," I say to my dad who's humming along to his favorite Beatles' songs. Static and loud voices screaming numbers echo from his police scanner. I wish he would turn that thing off once in a while.

"What? Why, Ashley?" he asks.

"I don't feel comfortable on the team." I say.

"Give me some facts, Ash. What exactly is happening that makes you feel uncomfortable and want to quit? You've never had problems feeling comfortable on a team before."

Give me the facts. He's always the cop.

"I don't know. I just don't feel right," I say. What should I say? Well, Dad, Christy is messing around with Mark and she hates me because Lizzy is my best friend, and don't forget, I'm selfish, blah, blah, blah.

"Instead, of just giving up, why don't you try to fix what's making you feel uncomfortable? If you can't fix it, then think about switching teams."

I chew on this. My attempt to fix this was kind of half-assed during Fall Brawl. I mean, Christy's hate for me runs pretty deep. It has to be more than just Mark and pitching. I flip open my cell, my dad continues to hum the oldies.

"Hey, Liz," I say while I stick hand over my ear to drone out the scanner and his humming.

"Hey, Ash. What's up?" Lizzy asks.

"What are you doing?" I have a pretty good idea what she's doing.

"Hanging out with Mark."

"Do you mind if I stop over?"

"Sure, we're at my house."

"Thanks, Liz. I'll be there in about a half hour," I say.

I lean back in my dad's seat, listen to "With a Little Help

from My Friends", mixed with my dad's humming, and scanner static and devise my plan.

"Hey, Ashley," Lizzy opens the door flushed red and disheveled. Obviously, she and Mark were squeezing in a hot and heavy make-out session before the third wheel arrived.

"Hi, Liz. Are you sure you don't mind?" I ask.

"No problem, Mark's down stairs."

I walk through the smoke-stenched dining room and down the basement steps. Lizzy's downstairs is really the first floor since she lives in a house on stilts. The downstairs is set up like a living room. A huge wrap-around black leather couch faces a television.

"Mom home?" I ask, but I know the answer.

"Nope. New guy," she answers.

Lizzy's mom had Lizzy at seventeen and married Lizzy's dad who was thirty-two at the time. By the time Lizzy was four, they split. Mom and Lizzy got the house. Lizzy hasn't seen her dad in like ten years. Lizzy's mom spends her days snoozing and her night's bartending at the Cape Town Tavern and picking up guys as a hobby.

Mark's lounging and playing with the remote. The Sports Center theme song plays in the background.

I plop down next to Mark while Lizzy grabs some snacks.

As soon as Lizzy is out of view, I pounce.

"Mark, I need to ask you something, between you and me."

"What, Ash?" Mark keeps his eyes glued to baseball spring training highlights.

"What is wrong with Christy?"

"What? Christy who?"

I lower my voice to a whisper. "You know what Christy I'm talking about. What is her problem with me? Did she ever say anything to you about me?"

"Maybe, once."

I scoot closer to Mark.

"What did she say?"

"She said something about how you kind of annoy her and something about your attitude," he answers still staring at Sports Center.

"Anything else? I mean the girl hates me," I say.

"No, nothing I can think of. I know she hates Lizzy with a passion, but that's obvious. Why do you care?" he chuckles.

I relax back into the couch. Why do I care? She has the right not to like me. Where do I get off thinking everyone has to like me anyway? I really need to stop obsessing over Christy. I've been spending all my time trying to figure out what Christy's problem is because I can't stand when someone doesn't like me.

Maybe Christy is right. Life isn't always about me, and not everyone has to like me. I bounce off the couch and barrel up the steps to join Lizzy.

Bottom of the Sixth
March, Freshman Year

"Are you ready for some softball?" I sing to Lizzy while we push through Sunray High's doors.

"You're way too perky for seven-thirty," she grumbles.

"Well, I had like the best weekend," I say.

I spent the last three days in Atlantic City cheering Jake on as he placed seventh in the State tournament. Kate and I took a forty-five minute bus ride courtesy of Sunray Beach High School. They ran a bus to States just so fans could cheer Jake on.

I'm so proud of him. It was awesome, seeing all his hard work pay off. I didn't really get to talk to him, but I did see him for a quick minute outside the snack stands right after his last match.

Finally, he can eat again. And eat he did. I swear he cleaned out a food stand all by himself.

Lizzy lets out a deep breath. She's still not thrilled about my friendship with Jake.

"You missed a great time. How's Mark?" I ask to change the subject.

"He's such a pain in the ass. I swear he's seeing Christy again. I'm so done with him. Even the so-called friends thing is so lame. I'm so done with him that I hooked up with this waiter, Tom, at my mom's job," she says.

I'm surprised at Lizzy for staying this long after snagging him with Christy in November.

"So, tell me about Tom." I cross my fingers hoping that this guy is under eighteen.

"Well, he's hot. He graduated from high school last year. Moved here from Pennsylvania. He's working as a waiter and going to school at night. My mom introduced us and we talked and stuff at my house after my mom's shift. He called me yesterday, but I'm done with guys for a while. So, I'm going to keep my options open."

Oh no, Lizzy, like so, so illegal.

"Sounds like a nice guy. Want to hang out at my house after practice? Girl's night," I ask. Hoping to get her away from becoming possible jailbait again.

"Sounds perfect." Lizzy answers.

"Why don't you stay the night?" I say hoping to keep her away from any more trouble her mom might bring home.

"Will your mom make my favorite chocolate chip pancakes

with the whipped cream?"

"Yeah, you know she'll do anything for you."

"I'm so there."

High school softball starts today and I'm back with a vengeance and a renewed focus. Things are starting to look up after a suck ass winter.

"Jenn, grab a mask. Ashley, grab a ball and start drilling in the batting cages," Coach Miller, Sunray's softball coach, instructs us during practice.

It's still frigid for March. I'm wearing two sweatshirts, a turtleneck, Under Armor, and sweatpants, but the artic coastal air cuts through everything.

One minor detail I so didn't even think of. The baseball field is adjacent to the softball field. I have a constant perfect view of Andrew Sinclair. Great.

"Can we switch?" I ask Jenn. I'm totally facing the baseball field, which means I'll be super tempted to look for Andrew.

"Sure," she grins. Jenn is a senior with platinum-dyed, blond, bobbed hair and brown eyes outlined with thick black eyeliner. She's a total Gwen Stefani twin. Jenn and the team treat me so sweet because they're all thrilled to have a decent pitcher this year. Cape Town only had four wins last year out of twenty-two games. Coach Miller's eyes lit up when she saw me pitch over the summer.

"Andrew and Zach, hit the batting cages, first," I hear the baseball coach yell in the distance.

Immediately, I tense up. My balls start losing velocity. I even launch one over the fence.

"Are you okay?" Jenn asks.

"Yeah, I'm fine," I lie.

I try to re-focus, but I hear Andrew and Zach dragging the pitching machine across the grass, getting closer with each step.

They begin to set up the pitching machine in the cage adjacent to ours. Why can't he just disappear?

I try to zone out Andrew, concentrating on Jenn's glove.

Snap.

"Wow, Ash, you're throwing hard," says Jenn.

"Thanks," I grin. Out of the corner of my eye, I spy Andrew watching me pitch.

I continue pitching and surprisingly, my concentration improves with each throw.

"So, Andrew how's Amy?" Zach asks.

I stop. Who the hell is Amy? Jenn throws the ball back to me, I stay as still as I can and stare at the ball in my glove.

"Whatever, man," Andrew answers.

"Come on, I saw you out with her last night, while Mark was all over that chick with the crazy blue eyes. I heard Cape Catholic girls are pretty easy." Zach chuckles.

Christy and Amy? Amy from Crush? Christy's best friend?

"Nothing happened man," Andrew says.

That's it. I can't stand it anymore. I say as loud as I can. "So, Jenn, what do you know about Jake Cole?"

"Huh?" Jenn says.

"Well." I say as loud as I can muster without shouting. "He made me like the most romantic dinner the other night. He's always thinking of me. Did you see him wrestle at States? Well, I did. We had such an amazing weekend. I'm so proud of him."

Andrew starts crushing the ball with his bat.

"What are you talking about?" Jenn looks at me like I'm from outer space. Pale blond strands stick up straight as she pulls off her mask.

"Nothing." I decide to stop talking because between the thump of the pitching machine and the clang of the metal baseball bat Andrew can't hear me anyway.

I continue to pitch. Why Amy? Out of all the girls in Cape Town, why one of my teammates?

I finish my workout with a speed drill. I love this drill. I am throwing so hard. Maybe I should paste Andrew's face on the catcher's mitt. I'll probably top off at 70 miles per hour.

When we're finished, I wait for Jenn so we can jog back to the field together.

"Are you really hooking up with, Jake?" Jenn asks.

"No, we're just friends," I say.

"So, that was all for Andrew's benefit."

I don't really know Jenn that well yet, so I lie. "Andrew was there?"

"You knew he was there. It's no big deal. First boyfriends are tough to get over."

I guess apple red face tells my story once again. I smile and join my teammates.

After practice, Lizzy and I decide to torture ourselves further and walk home in the freezing cold.

"So, what's up with Andrew and Amy?" I badger Lizzy.

"What are you talking about?"

I run down the batting cage incident.

"Are you kidding me? That's it, I'm done with that loser," Lizzy growls.

"What took you so long, anyway?" I ask.

"That jerk got under my skin."

"Girls night tonight, right?" Lizzy scowls as she flips open the phone.

"Before you call Mark. Make sure you ask him about Amy and Andrew."

"Get over Andrew. Guys suck," she shouts.

Here we go. A one-sided screaming match the whole walk home.

After a straight ten torrid minutes of listening to Lizzy tear Mark apart. I flip open my phone. No messages.

Jake doesn't believe in cell phones. He thinks that if you want to talk to someone, you should talk face-to-face. Especially, in a town as small as Cape Town.

The whole Amy thing is killing me. I need to know before practice this weekend. I need to know if he hooked up with her.

I press the button for Andrew. I can't do this. What am I going to say? I hang up. Seconds later, my cell phone rings. Oh no, he saw my number.

"Hello?" I answer.

"Hey, Ash. Did you just call me?"

"Uh. I must of pressed the wrong button. I was calling Jake," I lie hoping this will hurt Andrew as much as Amy kills me.

"Oh, okay. See you around." He disconnects.

Why did I say that? Before I chuck the phone into my bag I notice, I didn't shake. In fact, butterflies didn't even appear. Could it be? Could I finally be over Andrew? I mean, every time I even talked to Andrew, I totally freaked out, but he just caught me cranking him, and I didn't even shake. Nothing.

I start skipping toward my house.

"Hold on, Mark. Where are you going?" I hear Lizzy break from screaming and shout.

"I'll meet you at my house," I yell back. The frigid wind hits my teeth because I'm smiling so wide.

Girls night out doesn't exactly go as planned. Lizzy is so pissed at Mark we end up renting some chick flicks and hanging out in my room.

Lizzy and I are sprawled out on my carpet watching Cameron Diaz in the "The Holiday" when I hear sputtering outside, then my doorbell rings.

"Ashley, a boy is here for you," my mom yells.

Lizzy's eyes are huge. "He comes to your house?" she says.

"Every once in a while." I jump to my feet. "I'll be right back."

Jake stands in my foyer, clad in a UFC sweatshirt, jeans, and black boots.

"There's my girl," he says.

Footsteps echo behind me. Obviously, Lizzy and my mom.

"Hi Jake, what's up?" I say as I gently nudge him out the front door away from my audience. My socks freeze on the frosty ground.

"Do you want to go for a ride to celebrate your first day of softball?" he asks.

"Jake, that's sweet, but Lizzy's here," I say.

"Oh, no problem, I'll see you around tomorrow, then," he says.

Before I can say anything, he's gone, sputtering in the distance on his white and blue dirt bike.

My mom is standing at the door watching us. "Who is that strange boy?" she asks me as I walk back into the house.

"He's nice to me, Mom," is all I say. I turn the corner toward my room.

Lizzy sprawls back across the floor with an ice pack on her right shoulder.

"What are you doing?" I ask her.

"I'm beat up from practice, Ash. It's hard having to actually try-out. So, what did freaky boy have to say?"

"He's nice to me, Liz," I repeat. He is nice in a freaky sort of way. He cares about me and he's a friend. A friend who helped me get over Andrew.

Coach Miller is psyched about the season, so that means mandatory Saturday practices. Hey, I don't mind. I'm thrilled. More softball.

On my way home from practice, I spotted Jake's blue and white dirt bike parked against the fence at the skate park. Right after practice, I jump into the shower, do a quick make-up fix, and I'm off. I'm determined to pay Jake a visit after last night. That was so sweet of him to stop by.

A walk is refreshing on this warm March day. The wind and weather flipped over night, so it's not too frigid. Even though, it's only fifty degrees out, it feels like eighty after the winter we've had.

Five minutes later and I'm at the park. I spot Jake immediately by another Ultimate Fighting Championship long sleeve tee and black knit hat. He's riding his skateboard up and down a half pipe. When he reaches the top, he grabs the skateboard out from under him and replaces it just in time to skate back down the ramp. Then he skates up the other side. At the top he spins, once again landing just in time.

I had no idea Jake was a skater. Wrestling monster, yeah. But, skater? He's full of surprises. I can tell he's in the zone, like I am when I pitch. I know the look.

After fifteen minutes of staring, he notices me. He stops at the top and grins. With his foot, he flips the skateboard and catches it by his side. He carries the skateboard by its end and walks over to talk to me.

"Hi, Ashley." he says.

"Hi, Jake." I feel myself blush.

"What are you doing here?"

What am I doing here? I'm here because I've lost my mind again when I promised myself that I'd stop liking boys to focus on softball. I'm here because I'm a giant hormone and I regretted not kissing you on Valentines Day. I'm here because I'm finally over Andrew. And I'm here because I think I won't totally lose my mind with you.

"Returning the favor. You stopped over last night and asked me out. Now, I'm here."

"So, you're willing to go out with me again?" he asks.

Yes, you dumb-dumb.

"I guess." I say.

"I have just the place to take you. First, I have to stop at home. Hop on."

I follow him, wrap my arms around his waist, and take off.

Moments later, we pull up to a tiny bungalow, similar to Christy's house. Overgrown weeds border the foundation. Cement chips expose black marks. Normally, a house like this would freak me out, but with Jake I feel safe.

He coerces the dirt bike through the short green weeds growing through stones.

"Here we are," he says.

Wow, this is where Jake lives. I stare at the chipped paint and worn siding. A giant plant blocks the front step and I have to push past it to follow Jake up the steps. The screen door creaks open then slams shut. The living room looks more like a college dorm than someone's house. A tiny television sits on a beat up stand, two ripped, worn out couches face to frame the room. Old, scratched wooden floors spread out before us.

"What did you expect?" he asks. "It's just me, my brother, and my mom."

My expression must say exactly what I'm thinking. "It's cute," I say.

"Don't lie."

He plops down on one of the couches. "You know you're

the first girl to step foot in this house courtesy of me."

Finally, my chance to ask him about the girl rumors.

"All those girls you messed around with and you've never taken one to your house? So, how many did you mess around with, anyway?"

"Hi, Jake. Honey, how was skateboarding?" A woman enters the living room from the hallway. Her dark hair is full, full of hair spray. She's wearing black spandex, a leopard print top and holds a black cat in one hand with a cigarette in between her index and middle finger.

I'll have to slip in the girl or shall I say girls, question later. This is Jake's mom? I was expecting some rough and tough woman. This lady looks like a stripper.

"Hi, mom, this is Ashley," Jake says.

Jake's mom drops the cat. "Hi, Ashley. What a pleasure to meet you. I've read all about you in the papers. What a little athlete you are." She turns to Jake and her face turns sour. "She's a good girl, Jake. Don't screw this up."

"Whatever, mom." Jake takes off his knit cap and runs his hand through his buzz cut.

"You, ready, Ash?" Jake reapplies his knit hat and stands up.

"But, you just got here." Jake's mom stumbles into the arm of the sofa.

"Come on, Ash."

"It's nice meeting you," I say as I follow Jake out the door.

"Are you okay?" I ask Jake as he fumbles with his helmet.

"Fine, let's go for a ride." His serious expression switches to a grin. An easiness returns to his face once we're outside.

This time, Jake takes the back roads and we cross the bridge to the mainland.

He sharply turns into the woods and dodges trees. The trees open up to dirt hills.

After at least an hour of riding dirt tracks, Jake is cracking up. I must have screamed over every anthill. What a rush.

"You're a goofball," he says over his shoulder. He cuts the engine near a quarry. Crystal blue water fills a giant hole in the middle of the woods.

"I didn't even know this was here," I say.

"I spend a lot of time out of the house. I pretty much know where everything is," he says. He turns around and straddles the dirt bike seat to face me. Our thighs touch. Lightning strikes.

"Where's your dad?" I blurt.

"Gone," he says. "Never met him, or at least I don't remember him."

Poor thing.

"Oh," I say. I feel stupid asking.

"Mom's pretty bummed about my dad leaving. She never got over it. She does whatever to get by. Drink, smoke, drugs. My brother and I swear off the stuff. It just gets her into trouble. I guess that's why I wrestle. A lot of pent up stuff," he says.

His life totally sucks.

"What kind of stuff?"

"My life isn't like yours is, Ash. It's different. You never have to worry about if your mom's coming home. My brother is pulling in most of the money now just to keep our heads above water. My mom just sits on her ass all day drinking or doing drugs. You're lucky. Your parents are decent people. You shouldn't have a care in the world."

"Did you try rehab?"

"Of course we did. My aunt came down to the house a couple years ago and tried the whole intervention thing. My mom agreed to go then checked herself out of rehab in like two days. Six days later, she showed up at the house high again. What are we supposed to do, kick her out? She's our mom."

I can't help myself anymore, so I learn forward, close my eyes and kiss Jake. He kisses me back. It's rough, passionate and different from Andrew. He gently bites my lips and grabs the back of my neck pulling me toward him. I give in.

He stops kissing me, smiles, and stares.

"What?" I say.

"I just can't believe a girl like you is kissing a boy like me," he says.

At the moment, I start to open up and open up I do. I tell him about everything, Christy, Andrew, and softball. He listens for a long time, just letting me talk.

Then he says, "Did you ever think that Christy might be jealous of you? I mean, I'm sure it's hard to watch someone as pretty and talented as you with the perfect family and everything join her team and do as well as you have. As far as Andrew goes, I'm glad he dumped you." Jake smiles.

"That's sweet, not the jealousy thing, the Andrew thing."

He smiles.

I never thought about the jealousy thing before. Why would Christy be jealous of me? I'm a complete head case. Sure, my family is together, but my dad is an overprotective spaz, Max needs Ritalin, and my mom still talks to me like I'm six. Yes, I'm kept well fed, clothed, and warm so I guess I see Jake's point. Doesn't everyone take certain things for granted?

"Thanks for listening, Jake," I say.

"I'll always listen to you, Ashley."

He turns around and revs his engine. I grab a hold of his waist and he takes off with a jolt.

"What the hell do you think you're doing riding around on a street illegal dirt bike?" My dad's face is red. He's standing in the kitchen in full uniform. My mom is sitting at the kitchen table, a cup of coffee in front of her, nervously playing with her rings. When, Jake dropped me off around the corner, I thought it was strange my dad's patrol car was in the driveway. I knew this was his weekend to work. I had no idea one of the police officers saw me with Jake and called my dad.

"I didn't know it was a big deal," I say.

"If you didn't think it was a big deal, then why didn't you tell us about Jake?" my mom chimes in.

"Do you know what you are risking riding around with him? Not only your life, but everything you've worked for?" My dad looks like an over-inflated balloon ready to pop.

"Sorry," I say. I knew hanging around with Jake was risky, but it's fun. "I really didn't know the dirt bike was a big deal."

"You didn't think it was a big deal," my dad says. "First, you want to quit softball so you can hang out with Andrew. Now, you're riding around Cape Towne with a dirt ball on his dirt bike? Do you have any idea what type of family Jake is from? What is happening to you, Ashley?"

My dad begins to pace.

"We brought you up better than this," my mom adds.

What? At least I'm not Lizzy, messing around with a nineteen-year-old guy. Jake's my age, he's nice to me, and we have fun together.

"Look, I didn't know. Anyway, you don't know Jake. It's no big deal. We're friends. I won't go on the dirt bike next time," I plead.

"There won't be a next time. Ashley, you're done. Softball and school. That's it. Until you can get your priorities straight. You have a future Ashley. Start acting like the girl we know." My dad's arms are crossed.

"That's not fair," I say. Tears fill my eyes. "I am the same girl. I won't ever give up sports for a guy again. Andrew and I are over. Jake is a nice guy. What's wrong with me hanging out with a nice guy?"

"We are doing this for your own good, Ashley," my mom says.

"Whatever. You just want me to play softball. Well, guess what I'm more than just a pitcher. I'm more than just a college scholarship," I sprint into my room and collapse onto my bed.

I bury my face in my pillow. This is so unfair. They don't know Jake. They didn't know Andrew. I deserve a life. And I do finally have my priorities straight.

Top of the Seventh
April, Freshman Year

I pull my brand new yellow-striped white socks up to my knees. Over my head, I pull my brand new shiny golden jersey over my black Under Armor. Finally, above my sliders, I pull up identical yellow shorts.

This is it. Opening day. Today, we play our first high school game against Cape Catholic, me versus Christy. Today, Christy isn't an ASA teammate, she is the enemy. I can't wait to kick her ass.

We're home. So, I trek to the field adjacent to the high school. You can tell it's opening day. The field is well groomed with thick white lines and new orange dirt. Butterflies are back. After spending most of ninth period in the bathroom, there is nothing left in my stomach. So, I'm ready.

I spot a yellow bus make a turn onto our school's street.

Cape Catholic High School is scrawled across the side. This is it. My chance to prove to Christy, once and for all, not only am I worthy of starting over her on the Crush, but I'm better than her. Period.

Jenn looks my way as I stroll into the dugout. She's aware of how much this game means to me. We've been talking about it since we spotted the schedule.

"You ready?" she asks as she wraps her leg guards around her right leg.

"Yes, I am."

Last night, I spun the softball under my leg while I worked on a history paper. The night before, I spun while I finished my math homework. In between homework and spinning, I did speak with my window visitor. When you're punished, window visitors are a great pick me up. Plus, my parents didn't say I wasn't allowed to have guys at my window.

I grab the bright, brand-new, yellow ball balancing by itself on the end of the shiny silver bench.

I spin it into my glove as I wait for Jenn to finish strapping on her catcher's gear. The boy's field is vacant. They play Cape Catholic tonight under the lights. Andrew's home opener.

"Let's go," Jenn says.

We trot toward our warm-up spot, the cages. The rest of the team is taking infield.

I begin my warm-up. I stay in the zone throughout. So much

so, that only when I'm done do I realize Christy is warming up only ten short feet away from me.

"Hi, Christy," I coo.

She grins my way, but says nothing.

I may not be able to beat her with my mouth, but I will beat her on the diamond today.

I almost walk into a little old lady sitting in a lawn chair with a wool blanket pulled over her. White curly hair sticks out of a Cape Catholic visor.

"I'm sorry," I say to her.

"That's okay, dear. Are you Ashley?" she asks.

"Yeah," I answer.

"Nice to meet you. I'm Christy's grandmother. I've heard a lot about you from Christy. I hear you're a pretty good pitcher. Good luck, today." She holds out a pale, veiny hand.

What a nice lady. Why does Christy live with her and not her parents? I remember what Jake said. Is Christy's life like Jake's?

I shake her hand. "Thanks," I mutter.

Maybe Christy does play with my mind to try to secure her starting spot. Maybe Christy is like Jake, a fighter, fighting for her college scholarship because if she secures the spot, more colleges will see her pitch instead of me. One thing is certain, she'll never tell me.

I join my teammates and pair up with Jenn for some swings. Head down, I drill the ball into the silver fence.

Coach calls us to the dugout. On the way, Lizzy grabs my arm. "Hit her with a pitch today," she says.

Believe me, the thought has crossed my mind on numerous occasions, but after discussing it with Jake, tempting as it is, she is still my ASA teammate.

I hear a familiar sputter. It gets louder and louder. So loud, Coach pauses in between her pep talk because we can't hear her. Jake's making his appearance. I chuckle to myself. I look at Lizzy. She rolls her eyes.

"Okay, girls, let's do this. We've worked too hard to give up this game. All together."

We chant, "Cape Town," and scatter to our positions like children running toward their mommies after a day at preschool. I make the mound familiar, dig in, wind up, and release three quick pitches. I am ready.

The team huddles on the mound. "Team," we chant.

I sweep the front of the rubber with my foot. As I'm about to hollow it out, I scan the crowd. Next to the bleachers, my dad took a break from work and stands tall and proud in full uniform. My mom rests in her softball lounge chair next to him. Jake is far out in left field leaning against the fence. I spot Andrew and Mark sitting together at the top of the Sunray bleachers. I wonder if Lizzy notices this little speck of loyalty.

Cape Catholic's first batter, Stephanie, enters the batters box. She holds up her hand to the umpire, steps out to receive the sign, and then, digs in.

Jenn gives me the sign. Fastball outside. I shake my head. During ASA practice, Stephanie always smashes my outside fastball. Jenn smiles and looks at coach. Fastball inside and high. Better, less of a chance of a bunt.

I wind up and release. Stephanie leans into the pitch. It hits her upper arm.

The umpire tosses off his facemask and holds up his arms. She jogs to first.

Coach Miller explodes out of the dugout. She's waving her arms. After five minutes of arguing, she returns to our dugout. A few fans are still spewing sarcasm.

Obviously, Cape Catholic is going to do whatever it takes to win.

Next up, Amy. I wish she were the one who leaned into the pitch. It would have hit her in the face.

"Watch the steal," Kate yells from shortstop.

Jenn sets up outside and high. I wind up and release. Jenn jumps up and fires to second.

"Out," the infield umpire yells.

Stephanie jogs back to her dugout, staring at the ground.

"Nice one," I say grinning to Jenn.

Back to Amy. I look at Andrew to make sure he's watching. I wind up and fire a fastball.

"Strike," the umpire yells.

Emotions make me pitch, harder, faster. Jenn sets up for another fastball. She feels the velocity. I wind up and fire. Amy attempts to catch up with it.

"Strike."

Jenn looks at Coach Miller and once again sets up for another fastball. I wind up and fire. Stephanie makes minimal contact. Jenn squeezes the ball.

"You're out," the umpire shouts.

I smile as I receive the ball back and stare at Andrew. He smiles back at me.

It takes only three pitches to strike out Maggie. She can't catch up to my pitches. We jog back to the dugout.

Coach Miller calls out the line-up. "Lizzy, Ashley, Kate, Jenn." I'm shuffling my feet, full of adrenaline. I can't wait to get up to bat.

Lizzy grabs her brand new purple bat and slides on her helmet. "I'm going to smash the ball right in Christy's face." She says as she takes a few swings.

"Batter," the umpire calls.

Lizzy digs into the batter's box. Christy smiles, winds up, and fires, drilling Lizzy. Lizzy hits the ground hard immediately grabbing her knee. Coach sprints from the third base line to Lizzy.

I jog to the scene. Lizzy is spewing "F" words intermingled with Christy's name. The umpire looks down at the scene. Christy's catcher stands up to talk to her on the mound.

That's it. I can't stand it anymore. I yell, "What the hell is your problem? Can't strike her out, so you have to hit her? You're pathetic."

Coach Miller looks up at me from her squat next to Lizzy. "Ashley, knock it off. We need you today."

Christy's glove is in front of her mouth as she talks to her catcher. Her eyes crinkle.

The crowd claps as Coach Miller helps Lizzy to her feet. A purple welt covers her knee as she gingerly jogs to first base. The trainer returns to the dugout.

I'm so pissed off, I have to fight tears. I take a deep breath and turn toward Coach. She gives me the bunt sign. I want so badly to smack the crap out of the ball, but I think of the last time I ignored signs.

I dig in. Christy grins at me. She winds up and fires. I instantly recognize her rise ball. I let it go. The catcher can't handle it. Lizzy advances to second.

I turn toward Coach Miller. The green light. Nice. I dig in. Christy winds up and fires. Change-up. She gets me. I'm way ahead.

"Strike," the umpire yells.

She might have gotten me once, but not twice. I dig in again. Christy winds up and fires a fastball. I swing.

Smack. The ball finds a hole between shortstop and third base. I take off. Lizzy rounds third and scores. One to nothing. My

RBI. I'm jumping up and down on first base like a little kid. A flush of emotion takes over my body. Making eye contact with Jake, he smiles as he claps for me.

Kate grounds out, but I advance. Jenn hits a bomb to right field. Cape Catholic catches it, but I tag up and make it to third.

Casey is up next. She digs in.

"Come on, Case. Don't leave me hanging," I yell.

Christy releases a drop. Casey makes contact, but Maggie scoops it up at first.

We're flying high with a one to nothing lead.

I check on Lizzy. "Are you okay?" I ask her. The black lines under her eyes are smudged from crying.

"I'm fine", she says. Her knee is covered with a tan ACE bandage. "Let's just beat them."

"Go get 'em, Ash," Coach Miller says and smacks my back.

The game becomes a pitchers duel. Christy's got great control today and I'm firing harder, than I ever have.

Top of the seventh, the top of the Cape Catholic line-up is up once again. The score stands 1-0.

Stephanie digs in. She moves back in the box.

"Watch the drag," I yell to the infield. At third base, Lizzy creeps up toward Stephanie.

Jenn gives me the sign. I wind up and release. Stephanie's feet cross over. Dragging it down the third base line, she barely makes contact. Lizzy bare hands it and launches it to first.

"Safe," the umpire yells.

I hate when Stephanie's on. She's so fast.

"Watch the steal," Kate yells.

Amy digs in. She, too, moves to the back of the box.

"Drag," I yell.

Jenn gives me a low outside fastball sign. Good call.

I wind up and release. Amy juts out her arms to catch up with the ball. No contact. Jenn jumps up to stop the steal. She fires.

"Safe," the umpire yells as Stephanie slides into second.

"Let's keep her at second," Kate yells.

Amy digs in again. Jenn sets up for a change-up. I ease off and release. Amy recognizes my change-up and makes contact. The ball sails to center field. Our center fielder takes off running. She makes a spectacular over the shoulder catch, but the ball keeps her off balance. Stephanie easily advances to third.

One out. Stephanie at third.

"Let's keep her at third," I shout.

Maggie digs in. She looks serious, but flashes a quick grin. I grin back. Still friends.

I wind up and fire. Maggie squares to bunt. Jenn tosses her mask and grabs the ball, turns toward Stephanie at third. Stephanie's off the bag. Jenn fires the ball to Lizzy. Stephanie is caught in a run down. The ball sails back and forth until Stephanie headfirst dives back to third. Lizzy tags her helmet.

"Out," the umpire shouts.

"Yes," I shout and pump my fist. But, Maggie advanced to third during the run-down. Smart play. Two outs. Maggie on third.

"Get the out," Kate shouts. "Play's at first."

Christy digs in. Could it end any better than striking Christy out to end the game?

I look at Andrew and Mark. I glance at my mom and Christy's grandmother. I scan the bleachers for my dad. Where did he go?

My eyes meet Jake's in left field. I sway my foot back and forth and dig out the mound.

I set up on the mound. Jenn gives me the sign. High, inside fastball. I shake it off. She gives me another sign. I shake it off.

"Time out," Jenn yells. She takes off her face mask and meets me at the mound.

"Are you okay?" she asks.

"Yeah," I say. My hands are shaking. I feel I could like take off like a rocket ship. "I just want to set her up with a change-up, then fire the heat," I say through my glove, which I move over my mouth.

"You sure?" she asks.

"Yeah."

As she jogs back behind the plate. I glance at the stands

again. Get into your zone. My dad is gone. What? Why would he leave right now? A moment like this?

I wind up and release. Christy holds back.

"Strike," the umpire shouts.

Cheers erupt from the stands.

Jenn gives a fastball high outside. I shake her off. Low outside this time.

I wind up and fire. Christy can't catch up to it.

"Strike," the umpire shouts.

I think about Lizzy. I think about the Crush. I think about Jake and Andrew.

I tunnel all my hurt and anger into the next pitch. I wind up, fire, and release. She is miles behind it.

"Strike three," the umpire shouts.

The crowd explodes. My team surrounds me on the mound. We're screeching, screaming, and skipping. Even Coach Miller joins in the hysteria.

We line up to slap hands. Amy, Stephanie, and Maggie congratulate us. Christy congratulates everyone ahead of me, but skips me. Oh well, her loss. No really, her loss. I laugh to myself. I won. What a way to start the season. What a way to start ASA. Today, on this field it was proven, I'm better than Christy Mayer.

Bursting with delight and satisfaction, I gather my things. Jake is waiting for me by the dugout. Another set of dimples waiting for me. A new set of dimples. A better set.

I walk toward Jake, but within seconds, Andrew steps in front of Jake.

"Ashley, we have to talk," he says.

I'm shocked, Andrew hasn't said a word to me, minus Valentines Day, since December.

"Uh, right now?" I ask.

"Yeah, if you have a minute. I have something I need to get off my chest," he says.

"Hold on." I look around Andrew to find Jake to tell him I'll be right back. Jake is gone. I hear the roar of his dirt bike grow softer and softer in the distance.

My mom is standing next to Andrew.

"Great game today, Boo. I'm so proud of you." She kisses me on the top of my head and rustles my hair.

"Nice one, dork," Max says as he hangs on Andrew's arm. He still loves Andrew. Andrew grins and wrestles with him.

"Mom, where's dad?" I ask.

"He got a call. Some sort of accident or something. He'll be home later," she says.

My mom looks at Andrew, then me.

"I'll wait for you in the car," she says. "Come on, Max." My mom pulls Max from Andrew's arm. It takes a couple pulls. Max has one heck of a grip.

"Can we walk or something," Andrew looks at me with his great big brown eyes. On no, the old walk talk. The last time he asked me to walk, he broke up with me. What now?

"Look, Andrew. Whatever you need to say, just say it here. I really don't have all day." I switch my bag to my other shoulder.

"Look, Ashley. I thought I should clear some things up. Mark told me you thought I was hooking up with all these girls and stuff." He pauses. I stay silent. My ears hanging on every word.

"Well, I did hook up with Megan and Amy. But, I just wanted to tell you that I really liked you. The other girls are just girls. Hook-ups, no big deal. You were my girlfriend, you were special, and we had fun together. But, then you changed. It was too much, too soon."

"Changed? How did I change?" I ask.

"You quit basketball to hang out with me. It freaked me out. If I wanted a girl like that I would have dated someone else, like Megan. But, Ash, you were different. You had softball, soccer, and basketball. You were like me. You had a life. You were different. Then, you changed."

I stare at him. He meets my eyes. I can't believe that's the reason. All along, I thought he was banging Megan. So, he's blaming me. Blaming me for wanting to hang out with him. Whatever. Life isn't always about Andrew. Believe me, I've learned my lesson. Learned my lesson to stay away from guys like him.

I can't resist asking, "So, you never hooked up with Megan when we were together?"

"No, never. Like I said, I was into you," he says.

"So why did you hook up with her after me?" I ask.

"I don't know. What else am I going to do?" he says.

I take in Andrew's big brown eyes, broad shoulders, and thick chest. His Cape Town baseball hat is pulled low. He's right about one thing, though. His hotness made me nuts, blinded me, and I tried to change who I am for him. But, I can't believe I did that because when it comes right down to it, his personality sucks, and he's boring. I guess I was blinded by lust.

"Friends?" he says as he holds out his arms.

"Whatever," I say as I shake his hand instead. His eyes bulge to almost the size of his massive muscles and matching ego.

My mom is waiting in the car, engine idling. I have to find Jake. He's so good to me. So supportive. I feel terrible talking to Andrew instead of him. I rack my brain as I walk to the car.

"Mom, can I walk home today with Lizzy?" I ask. "It's been such a great day, I want to end it with my friends."

"I don't see Lizzy." She scans the fields. It's vacant, except for the grounds' men.

"She's in the locker room. She forgot something," I lie.

"Uh, okay. Just be home in an hour," she says.

"Thanks."

I toss my bag into the backseat. I have to make this right. I walk slowly toward the school. When I hear her car drive away, I take off.

Five minutes later, I arrive at the skate park. I check everywhere. No Jake.

I look down at my slides. Then, I check my watch. I slip off my slides and sprint toward Jake's house.

I make a right onto his street. The air burns my throat. I'm breathing heavy. A squad car is parked in front of Jake's house. What is going on?

I duck behind a tree, and I watch my dad walk out the front door. It squeaks then slams shut. His head is down. He gets into his squad car and pulls away.

Is he paying Jake some sort of visit? Is he warning him to stay away from me?

Jake's brother is next. He emerges from the house and sits on a beat-up chair on the porch. He puffs viciously on a cigarette and wipes his eyes repeatedly. A moment later, Jake storms out of the house and jumps off the porch.

"Jake," I shout. But, he keeps going. He must be really pissed at me.

"Jake," I shout again and take off toward him. He rolls his bike onto the street.

"Jake," I finally catch up to him. I'm breathless.

"Hi, Jake. I'm so sorry. Did my dad say something to you?"

He looks at me with tear-filled eyes. He looks pissed.

"Jake, what's wrong?" I ask.

"My mom. She's dead."

Bottom of the Seventh
May, Freshman Year

I haven't seen Jake since the day his mom died. Even though I begged, my parents wouldn't let me attend the funeral or the viewing because it was during school.

Poor, Jake. All I want to do is talk to him. Hold him. Tell him it will be okay. I miss him so much.

The rumors are swirling around Sunray. People are saying Jake's aunt took him in to live with her in a small town near Philadelphia and his brother is still living at the house. Or at least until the house is repossessed. I heard their mom had nothing; therefore, she left John and Jake nothing.

The day Jake's mom's died my dad came home from work early. He told me that Ms. Cole died of a drug overdose. John found her. Thank God, Jake was at my game and didn't have to witness the scene. It's terrible.

I started thinking about what it must be like to lose a parent. The earlier fight with my parents seemed so stupid after witnessing Jake's pain on that horrible day. My parents and I had a heart to heart and came to an agreement. With their help, I made a list, prioritizing my goals: family first, health second, religion third, schoolwork fourth, softball fifth, and my social life, sixth. But, at least, I had a social life again. Well, not really, after Jake left.

After spending a weekend in April, Googling drug overdoses and trying to figure out how I could find Jake, I finally figured out he was out of town and there was nothing I could do. Since Jake never owned a cell phone, there was no way to reach him. I also tried calling the house to talk to John, but the phone was disconnected. So, I threw myself back into softball.

Our Cape Town High School softball team qualified for the state tournament for the first time in ten years. We've enjoyed a great season, going 18 – 4. Even if we don't win one playoff game, all the starters are returning next year. So, I'm excited about next season.

My first ASA tournament with the Crush is this weekend. I'm looking forward to it, but a part of me can't stop obsessing about Jake's life. What is he going to do now? How is he going to afford to live? Will he ever come back to Cape Town? Of all people, even Lizzy is concerned about him.

"Are you packing, yet, Boo?" my mom shouts. "It's almost ten o'clock. We're leaving tomorrow at six in the morning."

Our first tournament is the Memorial Day Beach Blowout in Delaware. The weather is warm, so it should be a pretty nice weekend. I fold my clothes and place them neatly in my bag. I glance over toward my window and let out a shriek.

"Are you okay, Ashley?" I hear my dad yell.

"Yeah, just a bug," I answer. I'm smiling as I sprint toward the window and fling it open.

"Jake, are you okay? I've been so worried about you," I say.

Jake looks worn. His laid back look is replaced with a subtle sadness. His eyes are puffy. He's wearing a baseball hat pulled to the side.

"Hi, Ash. I missed you. I wanted to stop by to see you, again," Jake says.

I push open my screen and kiss his lips. They're warm and salty.

"Wow, Ash. I guess you wanted to see me too."

"What are you doing? Are you coming back? Do you have to live with your aunt?" I fire questions at him like a lawyer questioning a witness.

"Whooh, Ash. Slow down. One thing at a time. I'm here today. I might be gone tomorrow, but I'm here now."

"Wait right there," I say.

I zipper my bag, drag it onto the carpet, shove pillows underneath my bedspread, and lock my bedroom door. Hoisting myself up to the window, I duck through the opening then shut the window behind me and grab Jake's hand.

We sprint down the street toward the beach. As soon as we hit the sand, Jake pulls me to the ground. I take in his scent and kiss him hard.

"I missed you so much," he says.

"Me too, Jake."

We come up for air.

"Where are you living?"

He lays back on the sand and stares at the black sky.

"My aunt lives in this tiny town in New Jersey near Cherry Hill called Shady Maple. It sucks, and I'm new, and I hate it. But, they have a pretty cool wrestling coach and a good team. Plus, Coach is excited that I transferred and the town has a great skate park."

I take a deep breath. "Transferred? You're not coming back to Sunray?"

"Where am I supposed to live? John is barely making ends meet. He's going to put the house up for sale. He needs that money. Plus, like I said, Shady Maple has a decent wrestling team, so a better chance of a scholarship."

"Why can't your aunt move here?" I ask. Scanning my brain for ways to get Jake to stay in town, with me.

"My aunt grew up in Shady Maple. People that grow up in that town never leave. She loves it there and she'll never move down here. But, she is talking about buying a trailer in one of those vacation trailer parks on the mainland."

I lay my head onto his chest. "It's not the same," I say.

"It's better than nothing. And anyway, think of my luck. I finally get to hang out with you after all these years, and I have to move."

Jake's smiling ear to ear. "What?"

"Like you didn't know I've liked you since the third grade in Mrs. O'Donnell's class? I used to make you all these cards in art class."

I dig my elbow into the sand and balance my head on my hand. "Cards? I don't remember any cards."

"Well, I never really gave them to you." He pulls out multi-colored construction paper folded up into tiny squares and hands them to me. "I wanted to stick them in your desk, but I was too much of a puss."

I gingerly open the cards, reading each and every one. When I'm done, I kiss Jake over and over again.

"If that's what home made cards do to you, then I'll make sure I'll make you more."

We giggle, kiss, and stare at the stars until almost four in the morning.

I race home remembering I do have an ASA tournament

this weekend. Since my family didn't need me, my homework was done, church is on Sundays, softball is in two hours, and I feel damn good, it's time for a social life. And anyway, it's not like I'm skipping out on softball.

Acknowledgements:

Thanks a bunch to:

☺ Kim Mouldon, Amanda Mouldon, and everyone at FAST-PITCH FOREVER magazine and Blitz Publishing, Inc. for making my dream of writing a YA softball chick lit novel into a reality.

☺ My wonderful Word Warriors: Colleen, Angela, and Janice, you guys are the best.

☺ My amazing teachers, coaches, players, teammates, teacher buds, sporty buds, and writer buds that inspire me every day. A special thanks to Sandy.

☺ Nicole for being my freshman sports chick muse and first reader.

☺ Kelly, Karen, Ida, and my extended family for all of your encouragement.

☺ My much older brother for writing.

☺ My mom and dad for cheering for me on and off the sidelines.

☺ Sydney and Sabrina for making me smile.

☺ Justin for sitting through my first reads, providing a male influence, and your oodles and oodles of support. I know you secretly enjoyed the chick lit drama.

☺ Last, but not least, Kaci for just being Kaci.

About the Author

Keri Mikulski was born and raised in Maple Shade, New Jersey. She graduated from Thomas Jefferson University and earned a Master's degree from The College of New Jersey. She's the Chick Lit Pick columnist for South Jersey Mom magazine and contributes regularly to Fastpitch Forever Magazine. An athlete her entire life, she enjoys coaching her high school softball team, watching grannies pass her while running 5K's, chasing golf balls, Coach bags, and Derek Jeter. Keri lives at the Jersey Shore with her husband and daughter. This is her first novel. Visit Keri at www.kerimikulski.com.